SON OF A GUNMAN

**Center Point
Large Print**

This Large Print Book carries the
Seal of Approval of N.A.V.H.

SON OF A GUNMAN

Wayne C. Lee

CENTER POINT PUBLISHING
THORNDIKE, MAINE

This Center Point Large Print edition
is published in the year 2007 by arrangement with
Golden West Literary Agency.

The text of this Large Print edition is unabridged. In other
aspects, this book may vary from the original edition. Printed in
Thailand. Set in 16-point Times New Roman type.

ISBN-10: 1-58547-967-5
ISBN-13: 978-1-58547-967-2

Library of Congress Cataloging-in-Publication Data

Lee, Wayne C.
    Son of a gunman / Wayne C. Lee.--Center Point large print ed.
        p. cm.
    ISBN-13: 978-1-58547-967-2 (lib. bdg. : alk. paper)
    1. Large type books. I. Title.

PS3523.E34457S66 2007
813'.54--dc22

2006038161

I

It was the kind of day that makes a man forget that winter has just disappeared behind yesterday. Flowers were spreading color with wild abandon through the new grass over the rolling hills and bees were working industriously, trying to taste the nectar of every flower.

However, the balmy peacefulness of spring didn't penetrate the senses of Dusty Dekin and his hunch-backed companion as they crossed the divide between the two forks of Dreary River.

"That's a mournful tune you're playing on that squeeze box, Hunch," Dusty complained, looking across at his partner.

The hunchback rested his accordion on the horn of his saddle. "Sorry, Dusty. But that tune is coming from deep inside. I've got this feeling about what's ahead and I don't like it."

Dusty nodded silently. He'd ridden with Hunch Huckle long enough to have a healthy respect for his moods. They were often premonitions. Besides, he shared this feeling of impending calamity. They both knew they were heading for trouble when they rode into Jawbone.

"Does that feeling give you any idea what to expect?" Dusty asked.

Hunch shrugged his misshapen shoulders "It's just a bad feeling."

5

He began squeezing the accordion again, the tune reminding Dusty of a funeral dirge. Dusty frowned but said nothing. Riding into Jawbone under the present circumstances was bad enough without setting it to music.

They left the divide and began descending toward the north fork of the river, following a gully that had been cut by the run-off after dashing rains. As they broke out of the ravine onto a wide level bench above the slope running down to the river bottom, five riders suddenly erupted from a neighboring gully. Alarm tingled through Dusty but he smothered it as he saw the star on the shirt of the leader.

The riders pulled their horses to a sliding halt in front of the travelers. They spread out, two on either side of the man with the star. Dusty read the word "Deputy" across the top of the star.

"Are you Dusty Dekin?" the deputy demanded.

"So you've heard I was coming?" Dusty said softly.

"We've heard. But this is as far as you go."

"I have to see a man in Jawbone," Dusty said.

"You ain't seeing nobody in Jawbone."

The man on the deputy's right inched his horse forward. "Maybe I should fix him so nobody will recognize him if he does get to town."

Dusty stared at the man.

"That's Ben Lozar," the deputy said smugly, "in case you don't recognize him."

Dusty had recognized Lozar, all right, but he gave no indication that the name meant anything to him. Lozar was one of the fastest guns east of the Rockies.

He had also recognized the deputy, Zeke Torberg, from the description Charley Davis had given him when he'd told him about this job in Jawbone. The rest of the men were riding horses branded with a Big 'U'. That was Craig Usta's brand.

"I don't do business with hired guns," Dusty said.

Lozar snorted. "That's a good one! Matt Dekin's son has been hobnobbing with gun slingers all his life."

Dusty nodded. "That's why I don't do business with them."

"We know what they're here for," one of the Big U riders said. "Let's string them up and stop wasting time."

"There's a wagon down along the river," Lozar said. "If we prop up the tongue, that will do as well as a tree limb."

Dusty was watching the men closely. The deputy, Torberg, had started things off but now Lozar had apparently taken over as boss. None of the men had drawn his gun yet. That was probably because they had seen that neither Dusty nor Hunch wore a gun belt. Only one Big U rider was in a position to see the shotgun with very short barrels that Dusty carried in a special boot on the side of his saddle. The boot had little resemblance to a rifle boot and the shotgun's stock was almost hidden behind Dusty's leg. He could never get that gun in his hands, though, while Lozar was watching him so closely.

"They ain't playing scare-away," Hunch said softly to Dusty.

Dusty nodded slightly. He had expected trouble when he got to Jawbone but he had hoped to have enough time to ferret out and identify his enemies before he had to face them. Obviously Lozar qualified as one of those enemies and he or someone had primed these men for a hanging.

"Get that star off your shirt," Lozar said to Torberg. "We don't want the law involved in what we're going to do. This is a vigilante committee protecting our community."

"From what?" Dusty demanded as Torberg pulled the star off his shirt and dropped it into his pocket.

"From ruining the best cattle range in the state of Nebraska," one Big U man said. "If we let you get to town, several good men will be killed before this is settled. Hanging you two now will save a lot of lives."

Dusty glanced at Hunch. Somebody in Jawbone had talked too much and they'd said the wrong things. These men were fully conditioned for a lynching. Dusty caught Hunch's eye and saw his head barely nod.

"Do you figure we're here to kill cattlemen?" Dusty asked.

"That's the only reason Pettigrew would send for you," Lozar said. "But you won't be killing anybody once you stretch a rope."

Suddenly the comparative silence was shattered by a wheezing squall as Hunch lifted one end of his accordion. The five horses not used to that sound bolted away and their riders had their hands full qui-

8

eting them. When the horses had stopped prancing and their riders had wheeled them back to face Dusty and Hunch, Lozar was furious.

"Give me that infernal racket maker!" he screamed, nudging his horse toward Hunch.

He stopped short when Dusty's voice cut in. "Just stay where you are! The first man who makes a move will get cut in two with a load of buckshot."

The men stared at the sawed-off shotgun that Dusty was holding across the horn of his saddle as if it were a rattlesnake that had suddenly appeared from nowhere.

"You can't get us all with that," one Big U man blustered, breaking the dead silence.

"I can get two with each barrel the way this scatter gun sprays the shot. Which one of you wants to take the chance that he'll be the one who is left?"

"Nobody's making any foolish moves," Torberg said hastily. "Of course, you know we were only trying to scare you off. We wasn't really fixing to hang anybody."

"I'm glad to hear it," Dusty said drily. "Just drop your guns—very carefully. This thing has a hair trigger and I'm a nervous man."

Slowly each man unbuckled his gun belt and let it drop to the ground. Then the rifles were carefully slid out of their boots and dropped on top of the gun belts. With a wave of the shotgun muzzle, Dusty drove the riders back. Hunch dismounted and picked up the guns.

"What will I do with them?" Hunch asked.

"Load them on your horse," Dusty said. "These fellows aren't going to need them for a while." Slowly he moved the muzzle of the shotgun across the riders. "Get down and take off your boots."

"You ain't going to leave us afoot and barefooted, are you?" Torberg howled.

"Would you rather hang like you planned to swing us?"

The five men dismounted reluctantly and pulled off their boots. Dusty nodded at Hunch. The hunchback was back on his horse, his hands full of rifles and gun belts. Somehow he managed to pull on one end of the accordion again. As the wheezing wail cut through the meadow stillness, the riderless horses wheeled and galloped off toward town.

"Now the pants," Dusty said.

This brought another squall from the men punctuated by loud curses, especially from Ben Lozar. Dusty waved the shotgun menacingly and pants were unbuttoned and dropped.

Dusty swung down, keeping the shotgun on the men. "Let's have the shirts now."

Shirts were unbuttoned, each move punctuated with more curses. Dusty collected the shirts and tied the sleeves together, making an oversize pouch, something like a blanket. Into this he dumped the pants and boots and swung them all up behind the saddle on his horse.

"What do you expect us to do?" one Big U rider demanded.

"That's up to you," Dusty said. "Your pants and boots and guns will be in town. You can come after them whenever you feel like it."

"In our underwear?" Torberg screamed.

"Maybe I should take the underwear, too," Dusty said thoughtfully.

A barrage of curses filled the air. Dusty grinned.

"On the other hand, I doubt if that would add anything to the beauty of nature. You make a right pretty sight the way you are now. It isn't likely there are many people in Jawbone who have never seen underwear before. Let's go, Hunch."

Lozar, who hadn't said anything since he'd been ordered to take off his pants, glared at Dusty. "I'll kill you for this, Dekin! You can bet everything on that."

Dusty stared at the gunman. "This shotgun will be loaded for you any time you want to try it."

Dusty waited for the others to add to Lozar's threat but they all kept quiet. He nudged his horse across the bench and down the slope toward the river, Hunch following him. Curses broke out behind them but Dusty didn't even look back.

"They sure respect that scatter gun," Hunch said when they were half way to the river. "Would you really use that gun on them?"

"I have never fired a gun at a man in my life," Dusty said. "I saw enough of that when my Pa was living. Look what it got him."

"That bunch back there are liable to do anything now to get you," Hunch said.

"Whatever they do, it's not likely to be any worse than hanging us today, do you think?"

Hunch shook his head. "Reckon not. Do you suppose any of those fellows are the ones we're really looking for?"

"I doubt it," Dusty said. "Somebody in town must have guessed that we were coming to help the farmers put in their dam. That's why these fellows were out to stop us. Torberg and those Big U riders, at least, are local people. We're looking for one or maybe two or three killers who were in Kansas when my pa and your pa were killed."

"Maybe Ben Lozar is our man," Hunch said. "We're looking for a cold blooded killer and Lozar fills the bill. I figure that killer was after the money my pa was bringing home for my back operation. Your Pa got killed because he happened to be along."

"Maybe," Dusty admitted. "But it could have been the other way around. Matt Dekin made a lot of enemies while he was marshal of those trail towns. Maybe one of those enemies saw a chance to kill him. Finding that money your Pa was carrying was just a bonus."

Hunch was a few years older than Dusty but they had been almost inseparable since they'd taken the trail of the killers. They'd had very few leads until Charley Davis had come back from a trail drive to Montana and told about seeing Matt Dekin's watch in a jewelry store in Jawbone. It had been there for repair but the jeweler had refused to tell Davis who it belonged to.

"Was there any watches in those pants?" Hunch asked as if reading Dusty's mind.

"A couple," Dusty said. "But not Pa's. Charley said he read the inscription on the back of that watch the jeweler was fixing. 'To Matt Dekin from the town of Abilene.' If that watch is in Jawbone, the man who killed Pa is probably there, too."

"And so is the money that belongs to me," Hunch said.

"We've got more to watch out for than Lozar and the ranchers," Dusty warned. "The men we want here in Jawbone will probably know us but we won't know them."

The town of Jawbone was sitting right on the north bank of the river. There was a bridge across the river and the two riders clopped across it. At the end of the dusty main street, they stopped and Dusty dismounted, making a pile of the shirts, pants, boots and guns they were carrying.

Most of the business places of Jawbone were lined up on either side of the main street. The livery stable was closest to the river and half a dozen men were there now, clustered around some saddled horses that had come in riderless. Dusty didn't turn in. Until he got the feel of this town, he didn't want to be afoot.

North of the livery barn was a harness shop. Across the street from it was a feed store. To the north of the intersection from these buildings were two corner buildings, a bank and a general store. Beyond them, Dusty could see several buildings, the biggest ones being a saloon and a hardware store.

13

"Don't see no hotel," Hunch said.

"There's a two story building a block west," Dusty said. "That may be the boarding house Charley told me about. Looks like a school house just south of it."

As they rode through the intersection, a small dog leaped out and nipped at the heels of Dusty's horse. The horse jumped and Dusty yelled at the dog. But the little terrier continued to make dives at the horse's heels.

Dusty's hand fell on the whip that was coiled and tied with a thong to the side of his saddle. He had used that whip to crack the air over his mule teams when he had been freighting. Now he quickly flipped the knot loose and uncoiled the whip. With one snap of the leash, he kicked dirt in the face of the little dog and sent him ki-yi-ing out of the street.

The dog dodged behind the skirts of a girl on the porch of the general store. Dusty's eyes, following the dog, caught the girl's skirts and followed the dress up to her face. The fury in her dark blue eyes squelched his admiration for her fine features. Red hair showed under her hat. Under different circumstances, Dusty thought, those eyes could tell a man things that couldn't be put into words. Right now, however, the girl was having no trouble finding words.

"What kind of a fiend are you?" she snapped. "Beating a defenseless dog!"

"I reckon my horse didn't figure he was defenseless," Dusty said. "I could have taken the hide off him just as easy as kicking dust in his face."

14

"You ought to have the hide taken off you!" the girl retorted and whipped across the street, her skirts stirring the dust as she passed.

Hunch whistled softly after she was gone. "Must be the school teacher. She had some slate pencils in her hand and she's headed for the school house."

Dusty nodded. "She's a hot-headed one, that's for sure."

He reined over to the hitchrack in front of the bank and dismounted. It was the noon hour but maybe the banker would be in. His eyes ran up the street after the teacher before he stepped through the door.

Inside the bank, Dusty went to the window and asked the clerk for Phoebus Pettigrew. The clerk stared at Dusty for a moment then nodded toward a door at the far end of the counter. Dusty moved toward it, Hunch just a step behind him. At his knock, a shrill voice called for him to come in.

Stepping into the room, Dusty carried a mental picture of a well stuffed, over-fed banker, spilling over the sides of his soft chair. That picture exploded at the sight of Phoebus Pettigrew. The banker was a long thin man, over six feet tall and weighing less than Dusty did. Dusty guessed him to be between fifty and sixty years old with iron gray hair and piercing brown eyes.

"Dusty Dekin?" Pettigrew asked, his eyes flickering from Dusty to Hunch.

Dusty nodded. "Charley Davis told me about you. As soon as I got your letter saying you could use a

15

couple of good men to ride herd on things here in Jawbone, my friend, Joe Huckle, and I came."

"Mr. Davis recommended you highly," Pettigrew said then added, his voice skeptical. "Are you really Matt Dekin's son?"

"That's right," Dusty said. "Did you know him?"

"Saw him once in Abilene," Pettigrew said. "Two drunks were causing a ruckus and he cracked their heads together. Then when someone took exception to the way he was handling things and started to pull a gun, he drew and shot the man in the arm before he could squeeze the trigger. I never saw anything like it. Did he teach you how to handle a gun?"

Dusty nodded. "Sure. He told me a man had to be fast with a six-gun to survive. But I didn't agree with him."

Pettigrew's eyes searched Dusty like a lawman's well-trained hands. "You don't appear to be wearing a gun now."

"I'm not," Dusty said. "A six-gun sometimes invites more trouble than a man can handle. Look what it got Pa."

The banker stared at Dusty in disbelief. "The son of a gunman and you don't even wear a gun. You won't live twenty-four hours in this town."

"I carry a short barreled shotgun in my saddle," Dusty said. "They'd have thought I was going to rob the bank if I'd toted that scatter gun in here."

"What good is a gun when it's twenty yards from you?" Pettigrew demanded. "I thought I was hiring a fast gun to go against the gunmen Craig Usta is bringing in. I've got no use for a man who is afraid to wear a gun."

"You hired me to do a job," Dusty reminded the banker testily. "How I do it is my business. Just give me the details of the job and I'll take care of it."

The banker sighed, disappointment and hopelessness written plainly in his face. "Funeral expenses are not included in your wages."

II

Dusty could see that no amount of confidence on his part was going to rub off on Phoebus Pettigrew. Pettigrew was a man who wanted solid collateral for his loans and now he wanted more proof than an empty handed gunman that Dusty could handle the job he wanted done.

Dusty's confidence was shaken as he watched the banker. According to Charley Davis's evaluation of the situation here at Jawbone, a gunman's reputation was all that would be needed. Dusty had traded on Matt Dekin's reputation more than once. He wasn't sure it would work here. That episode south of the river this morning had been a warning that it wouldn't.

He glanced at Hunch. The hunchback was evidently thinking the same as Dusty. But like Dusty, he had some important things to find out here in Jawbone, and the situation was going to have to get much stickier

17

than it was now before he'd tuck his tail and run.

"Just what do you want me to do that is going to require a gun?" Dusty asked.

"Be town marshal for one thing," Pettigrew said.

Dusty's eyebrows went up. "You've got a deputy sheriff. At least, I suppose Torberg makes Jawbone his headquarters."

"He goes," Pettigrew said. "The sheriff is over at Taylor, the county seat. He seldom shows up here. Torberg is the only law we've got and that's worse than nothing."

"He's not going to sit still for a town marshal," Dusty said.

"I don't expect him to. That's why I wanted a man who wore a gun and wasn't afraid to use it."

"You can't have two lawmen covering one area," Dusty said.

"This town is incorporated," Pettigrew said. "So Torberg has no jurisdiction inside the city limits if we have a town marshal."

"You and who else planned to make me marshal?" Dusty asked.

"The town council. I'm mayor of Jawbone."

Dusty nodded. He just hadn't figured Pettigrew for a man who dabbled in anything that required cooperation with the local citizens.

"In the absence of a marshal, doesn't Torberg have control of the town?"

Pettigrew nodded. "Exactly. And that's one thing we want stopped. Torberg is Craig Usta's man."

It was Dusty's turn to nod. Now they were getting down to the meat of things.

"You want me to buck Zeke Torberg and that fast gun, Ben Lozar."

"You're finally getting it."

"You're finally getting around to saying what you want," Dusty said.

Pettigrew leaned forward. "The farmers are going to put a dam across the river to the west of here. With that, they can irrigate the flat land below the dam. They'll bring in many more farmers and this will be one of the most prosperous areas of the state."

Dusty nodded. "And the ranchers are afraid those farmers will spread right out into the hills and tear up the grass there, too, once they get in the country."

"Something like that," Pettigrew acknowledged. "The ranchers also use this river grass for winter hay. But they can't stop progress. The farmers who are already here have formed an association to build the dam. They have sold shares to people who will move in later and have borrowed enough money to build the dam. The money is coming in on the stage tomorrow. If you take the job we brought you in to do, you'll be guarding that money."

"I took the job as soon as I got your letter," Dusty said. "You're the only one who seems to doubt that."

Pettigrew stared at Dusty and Hunch, who had been sitting back to one side without saying a word. "I should think you would know by now that this is not a job for a man afraid to use a gun."

"Can't say that I've seen any men around who are afraid to use a gun," Dusty said. "Trying to avoid a fight doesn't mean a man is afraid."

"We'll let the town council decide that," Pettigrew said.

"When does the council meet?"

"This afternoon. You'd better be here. It will also be your job to protect the contractor who has agreed to build the dam."

"Wait a minute," Dusty protested. "That dam isn't going to be built inside the city limits and you said that was the territory of the town marshal."

"The contractor has his office here in town. In fact, it's right in the back of this building." Pettigrew got up. "Come on. I want you to meet him."

Dusty and Hunch followed Pettigrew to a door in the back of Pettigrew's office. The banker rapped on the door and was greeted with an invitation to come in. The three men went through the doorway.

A man with bushy red hair was sitting at a desk facing an outside door. His desk was cluttered with papers and some books. A couple of maps were spread on top of the mess and Dusty guessed they were survey maps of the area where the dam was to be built.

They had come into the office from the side and now Pettigrew led them around to some chairs in front of the desk.

"This is Vyrl Wolfe, the engineer who has contracted to build the dam," Pettigrew said. "Vyrl, this is Dusty Dekin and his sidekick, Joe Huckle."

Dusty and Hunch acknowledged the introductions and Dusty noted Wolfe's eyes sweep over him, apparently looking for his gun.

"I'm glad to meet the son of Matt Dekin," Wolfe said, holding out his hand.

Even as Dusty shook hands with the engineer, he noted the look of doubt in his face. Normally there was doubt and apprehension among people who met a man wearing a gun. Here in Jawbone, it was reversed.

"The situation here could get out of hand if Usta is allowed to go too far in harrassing our operation," Wolfe said.

"So I gather," Dusty agreed. "It seems I am not hired yet. The final decision is going to be made by the town council."

"A reputation isn't going to be enough to stop Usta," Pettigrew said. "We need a man with a gun."

Wolfe stared at Dusty a moment then switched his gaze to the banker. "Have you got anything better in mind?"

Pettigrew frowned. "No. But this situation requires decisive action."

Wolfe nodded. "We might get it from this man even if he doesn't wear a gun."

Dusty felt like a horse in an auction ring as the two men discussed him. "I'd rather have a job freighting-in supplies for your dam," he said. "I've been driving freight wagons for a long time."

"I'll keep that in mind," Wolfe said. "But there's a bigger job to be done. I'm not convinced as Mr. Pettigrew seems to be that you're not the man to do that job."

Dusty liked Vyrl Wolfe and it wasn't just because he seemed to have confidence in him where Pettigrew didn't. Wolfe struck Dusty as a solid man who wouldn't be easily shaken out of a conviction.

As Pettigrew led Dusty and Hunch back into the bank, Dusty asked him about any newcomers who had showed up in Jawbone recently.

"There are plenty," the banker said. "Ever since word got out that a dam was going to be built, speculators have showed up. And Usta has brought in some gunmen, headed by Ben Lozar."

"Any of these tough hands come from Kansas?"

The banker shrugged. "It's possible. Kansas isn't so far away."

"Is there a jewelry shop in town?" Dusty asked.

"There was, but the jeweler didn't like the caliber of people moving to Jawbone so he packed up and left. Said it wasn't safe to run a jewelry shop where there were so many outlaws."

Dusty nodded, hiding his disappointment. "He could be right."

"Don't forget that town council meeting in an hour," Pettigrew said as Dusty and Hunch prepared to leave. "It will be right in this office."

Outside the bank, Dusty stopped at the hitchrack in front of his horse. "We'd better get us a room, Hunch," he said.

"I hope it doesn't take us long to find the man we're

looking for," Hunch said. "I don't like the feel of things here. There's going to be one dirty fight if those farmers are dead set on building a dam."

"They seem to be," Dusty said, "or they wouldn't have hired themselves an engineer."

Hunch nodded and ducked under the hitchrail to his horse. "How long do you figure it will take those half-naked jaybirds we left out south of the river to get to town?"

"I look for them to make it about the time the town council meets," Dusty said as he reined his horse up the side street.

The boarding house was a block west of the main street and took up a position almost in the center of the block facing the street. It was a big square two-story house painted white but the paint was now beginning to flake and peel off. The grass that had been growing in front of the house was beaten down by men who wouldn't take time to follow the laid-out path.

On a small porch that occupied the southeast corner of the house was a big bucket of water and two wash basins and a half dozen towels in various stages of griminess. In front of the screen door was a mud puddle where the water from repeated face and hand washings had been dumped.

Dusty and Hunch stepped around the puddle and went through the door onto the porch. Dusty rapped his knuckles on the door that led from the porch to a big parlor.

A huge woman came to the door, wiping her hands

on her apron. "Glory be!" she exclaimed. "Ain't often I find anybody bothering to knock before coming in. Step inside and let me look at some gentlemen."

Dusty and Hunch went through the door into a room that was as spotless as the front yard was sloppy. Two divans and a half a dozen chairs were in something of a circle around the room. Through a door to the right, Dusty could see a kitchen that appeared as spotless as the parlor. Next to the kitchen was a room with a long dining table and more than a dozen chairs. A stairway led up from the far end of the parlor.

"We're looking for a room," Dusty said.

"You're looking in the right place," the woman said in a booming voice. "I'm Molly Guzek. I've got the only boarding house in town. And there ain't no hotel. I've got just two rooms left. You can have your choice. Fifty cents a night or three dollars a week."

"We'll take one for a week," Dusty said. "I'm Dusty Dekin and this is Joe Huckle, just in case someone comes looking for us, which ain't likely."

Hunch shot a glance out into the street. "I'm not so sure about that. There are some pretty mad jaspers walking barefooted in from south of the river about now."

Molly's eyes lighted up. "Who's walking barefooted?"

"Your deputy sheriff and four fellows riding Big U horses," Dusty said. "One of them is Ben Lozar."

Molly whistled softly. "When you tie a knot in a tail, you pick the ringiest steer in the herd, don't you?"

"I haven't had a chance to look over all the herd yet," Dusty said. "Just which one do you figure is the ringiest?"

"Ben Lozar," Molly said quickly. "He stays here so you'll get to see him plenty. Now I want you to understand—I won't have any shooting here at my boarding house."

"I don't even carry a gun," Dusty said innocently.

"That ain't going to stop Ben from fanning some lead if you have set him afoot without any boots."

"Or pants or shirt," Hunch added.

"Oh, glory!" Molly breathed. "Maybe I shouldn't even let you have a room."

"You don't want us sleeping in the livery barn, do you?"

"I don't mind you sleeping here. But I don't want it to be a permanent sleep."

"Any other special guests staying here?" Dusty asked.

"According to who you call special," Molly said. "You don't need any more special friends like Lozar. Serg Sitzman, the gambler down at Gumpy's Saloon, stays here. And the engineer, Vyrl Wolfe. His men camp out but he stays here."

"You have quite a collection," Hunch murmured.

Molly's eyes suddenly twinkled. Dusty had never seen such expressive eyes as the huge owner of the boarding house had.

"I've got someone else here that you boys will enjoy. The school teacher, Jennie Blair."

25

Hunch grunted and Dusty frowned. "Is she a red-head?" Dusty asked.

Disappointment registered in Molly's face. "Have you met her already?"

"I'm afraid we have," Dusty said. "She won't like us any better than Ben Lozar does. We ran afoul of her dog."

Molly shook her head. "If you scolded her dog, she'll hate you forever."

"Does she take that dog to school with her?" Hunch asked.

"She takes him everywhere with her except to bed. She'd do that, too, I guess, if I'd let him in the house. He's got his own little house at the back door. Come on up and look at your room."

"How long have you been in Jawbone?" Dusty asked.

Molly started up the stairs. "Ever since there was a Jawbone," she said. "This was the south end of our ranch that ran back into the hills. Jim built this big house for me. He was a wonderful husband until somebody killed him. He just rode out to work on the ranch one day and didn't come back. Took the sheriff two days to find him. He'd been dragged to death. They ruled it an accident but I know better."

At the head of the stairs, Molly turned down the hall and stopped at the third door. "This is the best room I have left," she said. "Jim built a bigger house than I thought we needed. But it sure has come in handy since I've had to do for myself."

"What happened to your ranch?"

"Craig Usta bought it. I just kept this house and two acres here on the edge of town."

Dusty and Hunch went inside and Molly followed them. There was one bed and one window. A dresser was behind the door when it swung back. There was only one chair and the mirror was cracked. But the room was clean. The big pitcher and bowl were also spotless.

"Ever hear how Jawbone got its name?" Molly asked and without waiting for an answer proceeded to tell them. "Jim was digging a post hole one day and dug up the jawbone of some poor fellow who'd been dead a long time. Some of our neighbors heard about it and said we should call in some educated professor to tell us how long the fellow had been dead but Jim said he wasn't going to be no party to grave robbing so he put the bone back where he found it and buried it again and never told nobody where it was. But people started calling our place the jawbone place and when a town started right here on our ranch, naturally it was called Jawbone."

Dusty had never run into anyone who liked to talk better than Molly. But he decided that could be a good thing for him if he just stayed on the good side of her. He doubted if there was much that went on in or around Jawbone that she didn't know.

"We've been hearing about the farmers building a dam on the river," Dusty said. "Is there going to be trouble?"

Molly put both hands on her hips and glared at Dusty. "If you haven't heard about that trouble, you're an idiot for being here. Pettigrew sent for you, didn't he?"

Dusty nodded. "He didn't tell us much about what he wanted us for."

"Old Tight-mouth wouldn't," Molly said. "He wants you to kill off a whole passel of ranchers, I reckon, so the farmers he's loaned money to can build their dam and irrigate the bottom land. Then Pettigrew will get rich."

"If you think I'm here to help the farmers, why are you letting me have a room?"

"I figure your money is as good as anybody's. Anyway, I can't say that the ranchers are all smelling like daisies. They've brought in some pretty shady characters like Ben Lozar. They've borrowed money to have cash to pay this crew of gunmen. I hear they're going to keep their money in Tom Nettles' store because they don't dare put it in Pettigrew's bank."

"How can a storekeeper take care of so much money?"

"Nettles has a safe in his store. That safe was the only bank Jawbone had till Pettigrew moved in. But with the ranchers' money there and the bank holding the money the farmers are bringing in to pay the contractor, this town is going to attract robbers like a clover patch draws bees."

"Looks like we're sitting in on a pretty hot game, Dusty," Hunch said. "If we're going to play, we've got to get down to that meeting Pettigrew called."

"Farmers' meeting, I reckon," Molly said, eyes flipping from one to the other.

"It's a town council meeting," Dusty said. "Pettigrew is trying to decide whether he wants a town marshal who doesn't carry a gun."

Molly nodded. "He could be showing more sense than usual."

"We'll probably be back for supper," Dusty said. "We won't bring in our gear till we find out whether we're going to stay."

The town showed no more activity than before as they rode back to the bank and tied their horses. Going through the bank, Dusty knocked on Pettigrew's office door. Pettigrew's invitation to come in sounded weak to Dusty and a warning tingled through him.

But apparently Hunch didn't notice anything strange for he reached around Dusty and turned the knob, pushing the door open. As the door swung back, Dusty saw Ben Lozar standing squarely in front of him, fully clothed now and with his gun strapped around his waist.

Dusty didn't doubt what was on his mind.

III

Dusty stared at Lozar and quickly collected his thoughts.

"I didn't know you were on the town council," he said.

"Where's your gun?" Lozar demanded.

"I never carry one," Dusty said. "A fellow can get in trouble packing a gun around."

"You don't think I'm going to let you get away with what you did, do you?" Lozar demanded.

"Hadn't really considered it," Dusty said, realizing that Lozar was not so sure of himself now or he would be shooting, not talking.

"I'm going to kill you!" Lozar roared, trying to drive himself into a frenzy. "Just because you haven't got a gun don't matter."

"I'm not stopping you. But there *are* going to be a lot of witnesses."

Dusty glanced at the three men besides Pettigrew who were in the room. Lozar flicked his eyes around, too. Finding himself in the role of murderer instead of that of an injured party seeking justice was shaking his confidence.

"If you've got a lick of sense, Ben, you'll get out of here while you can," Pettigrew snapped.

Lozar wheeled on the banker, looking for a place to vent his frustration. "Keep your nose out of this or I'll blow *your* head off, too."

Hunch slipped past Dusty and moved to the opposite

side of the gunman. As he shuffled to the far side of the room, Lozar's eyes followed him. This put his back partly to Dusty. Dusty had worked too long with Hunch to miss the opportunity his partner was giving him.

Stepping forward quickly, he reached out and flipped Lozar's gun from its holster. The gunman squalled like a wounded cougar and whirled back. But Dusty was holding the revolver carelessly in his hand and Lozar was unarmed.

"Seems I have to keep taking this thing away from you," Dusty said softly. "I may have to give this to someone for safe keeping."

The veins stood out in Lozar's face as he fought his fury. "You just keep it and be wearing it the next time I see you."

Dusty held up his hand. "Everybody knows I don't carry a gun. I won't carry this one, either."

"I'll—I'll kill you, anyway!" Lozar raged. "I'm giving you warning!"

"We'll have a rope ready for you if you kill an unarmed man," one of the men across the room from Dusty said.

Lozar glared at the man, then turned his frustrated fury on Pettigrew and Dusty. Finally, with a curse that was almost a blubber, he dashed out of the room, slamming the door so hard it quivered on its hinges.

"Never thought I'd see Ben Lozar cowed by a man without a gun," the man across from Dusty said.

Dusty grinned, mostly in relief. "I've got his gun but

I don't want it. Will you keep it, Mr. Pettigrew?"

He handed the gun to the banker, who took it reluctantly. Pettigrew laid it on his desk then turned to the other man.

"This is Dusty Dekin, gentlemen, in case you haven't already guessed, and his sidekick, Joe Huckle. Dusty, this is Ed Klosson, a farmer who has settled about two and a half miles above town. I've asked him to sit in on our town council meeting today."

Dusty shook hands with the man who had taunted Ben Lozar. He was a blond blue-eyed man with a big frame, almost as tall as Dusty and thirty pounds heavier. Dusty decided that nothing would ever scare Ed Klosson, not even death.

"This is Serg Sitzman," Pettigrew said, motioning to the next man. "He's on our council."

Dusty turned to Sitzman. He was younger than Klosson and smaller but given to an excess of flabby fat. His squinty eyes seemed sunken in folds of fat but they were so sharp that Dusty could almost feel their penetration.

"He didn't tell you that I make my living gambling over at Gumpy's Saloon," Sitzman added as he took Dusty's hand.

"I know," Dusty said. "We took a room at Molly Guzek's."

Sitzman nodded. "Then you should know everything about everybody in town by now. No need of any introductions."

Dusty turned to the other man, a short heavy-set

man, bald with piercing gray eyes. Dusty decided the reason Sitzman didn't look fatter was because he was standing by this man who was six inches shorter than Dusty and outweighed him by at least sixty pounds.

"This is Fred Yoeman," Pettigrew said. "He owns the hardware store and is also on our town council."

Yoeman shook Dusty's hand but he spoke to Pettigrew with a shrill wheezy voice. "Looks to me, Phoebus, like this young fellow has just proved himself. Anybody who can handle Ben Lozar without a gun should be able to handle the whole town."

Dusty could see that Pettigrew had lost much of his doubt he'd had when Dusty and Hunch had been in his office earlier. Ed Klosson added his vote of approval.

"I'd say he's got Lozar's number now. Lozar ain't above shooting a man in the back but he will hardly dare do that now. If anything happens to our new town marshal, Lozar will know he's going to have to answer for it."

"Lozar's not the only man the ranchers have who is capable of shooting an unarmed man," Pettigrew warned. "However, I believe Dusty is the man for our job. Maybe the fact that he doesn't carry a gun will prove to be the strongest weapon of all."

The door burst open and Zeke Torberg strode in, his clothes, gun and deputy star all back in place.

"I hear you're fixing to appoint a town marshal," Torberg said, trying to ignore Dusty and Hunch. "I'm warning you. I'm deputy sheriff here and I won't tolerate any shenanigans like this."

"This town is incorporated," Pettigrew said sharply. "We have every right to appoint a town marshal. Your jurisdiction is outside the town limits; his will be inside."

Torberg glared at Pettigrew then at Dusty. "I'll see the sheriff about that. But even if he is allowed to tote a badge in town, he'd better not stick his nose outside the town limits. I'll *kill* him."

"You're supposed to be a law officer," Klosson snapped. "You're talking like the hired killer you really are."

Torberg wheeled on Klosson. "This jasper stripped me of my boots and pants and shirt and made me walk three miles to town after them. Now would *you* feel like kissing him if he'd done that to you?"

Klosson couldn't keep the grin off his face. "I reckon I wouldn't. But I wouldn't go spouting off about how I was going to kill him, either. I figure you did something to deserve what you got. You're always flashing your gun around. Where was it when he was stripping you?"

Torberg glared at the circle of men for a moment then wheeled and slammed out of the room with almost as much fury as Lozar had shown.

"We seem to be of one opinion," Pettigrew said after the deputy had left. "Meet our new town marshal."

Pettigrew picked up a marshal's badge and stepped around the desk. He pinned it on Dusty's shirt.

"I figure you've got more in mind for me to do than just tote this badge around town," Dusty said.

34

"We have," Yoeman agreed, stepping up beside Pettigrew's desk. "As you know, the farmers have contracted with Vyrl Wolfe to build a dam across the river above here. That will bring in more settlers and it will mean prosperity for the town. But it will cost a lot of money. That money will be coming in tomorrow. We expect you to make sure the ranchers don't get it."

"Do you think they'll rob the bank?"

"If they don't take it before it gets here," Pettigrew said.

"If they try to take it before it gets to town, that will be Torberg's job to protect it. My jurisdiction won't go beyond the town limits, you know."

"We don't expect you to limit your activities to the town when it comes to protecting such things as that money shipment," Pettigrew said.

"I'm going to make Hunch my deputy," Dusty announced.

"With our blessings," Pettigrew agreed and produced another badge.

"I'd keep my eye on Lozar and Torberg if I were you," Klosson said as the men prepared to leave the office.

"Keep away from that red-headed school teacher, too," Yoeman warned Dusty. "Torberg thinks he has the inside track there. As touchy as he is now, you could get shot if you rub his fur the wrong way."

Dusty grinned. "I'm not liable to crowd him where the teacher is concerned. She's ready to shoot me herself."

"What did you do to her?"

"Kicked some dust in her dog's eyes with my whip."

Klosson grinned. "You might as well slap Jennie as scare her dog, Napoleon."

"So I found out. Think I'll go out and look over my new territory."

Dusty walked back through the bank and out into the street, Hunch just a step behind him. It would soon be closing time for the bank but the stores would be open for some time yet.

"We're getting awful involved in this town's troubles," Hunch said softly. "We didn't come here to cure Jawbone's sickness."

"I know," Dusty said. "But sometimes the only way to gather information is to get involved in what is going on."

"We're involved, all right. Wonder if anybody here knows where that jeweler went."

"Unless it is within a half day's ride, it wouldn't do us any good to know," Dusty said. "We can't take time to look him up. Besides, whoever had Pa's watch probably lived right here in Jawbone or on some farm or ranch close by. I'm betting he's still here."

"I'm just living for the day when I can find him," Hunch said. "Let's see what's in the stores."

They headed up the street away from the river. A land office was next to the bank, getting ready for the great influx of settlers when the dam was built, Dusty guessed. Next to the land office was the hardware store that Fred Yoeman owned. Beyond it was a restaurant and across the street from it was a barber shop.

At the hardware store, Dusty and Hunch crossed the street to the saloon. Dusty looked in over the swinging doors but didn't go any farther. The place appeared to be almost empty.

Going back down the street, he passed the deputy sheriff's office with a jail in the back then stopped in front of the grocery store which was directly across the street from the bank.

"We got to the boarding house too late for dinner," Dusty said. "Some cheese and crackers would go pretty well right now."

"I've been wondering if we were ever going to put on the feed bag," Hunch said.

The interior of the store was dim. A little man, obviously the operator, met them a few feet from the door.

"Can I help you?" he asked.

Dusty got the impression that he'd rather be anywhere than where he was and he wondered if he was nervous like this all the time.

Then Dusty saw another man farther back in the store and he understood why the storekeeper was so nervous. Ben Lozar was leaning against the cracker barrel half way to the back of the store and he was glaring at Dusty.

"Tell me what you want and I'll get it," the storekeeper said quickly.

Dusty looked at him again. This had to be Tom Nettles, according to what Molly had told him. Right now he just wanted to get Dusty out of the store before he and Ben Lozar tangled. Dusty had the feeling that nothing Nettles could do would prevent a clash between him and the gunman.

"Still a yellow belly?" Lozar said, pushing away from the barrel. "Afraid to wear a gun?"

Nettles wheeled back toward the gunman. "Now, Ben! Don't start anything."

Lozar pushed past the storekeeper. "He started it out south of the river this morning. I'm going to finish it right now."

"Just how do you expect to finish it?" Dusty asked softly.

"Since you're too big a coward to fight like a man, I reckon I'll have to whip you like I would a kid. Only I'm going to kill you with my bare hands." He unbuckled his gun belt and let it fall.

Dusty breathed easier. He had seen that Lozar had found another gun and he hadn't been sure that he wouldn't use it then claim self-defense, figuring Tom Nettles would be too scared to tell the truth later. He'd have to kill Hunch, too, but that wouldn't cause a killer like Lozar to lose any sleep.

Dusty had been in many fistfights. Being the son of Matt Dekin and not carrying a gun, he'd had to defend his right not to be called a coward many times. Ben Lozar was ten pounds heavier than Dusty but he was several inches shorter. Dusty was confident as Lozar charged at him.

Ben Lozar was not the lunging, wild swinging

fighter Dusty had expected. Somewhere he had learned the art of boxing and Dusty, using his own skill as a boxer, found the gunman harder to hit than he had expected.

But Dusty's longer reach got in some stinging blows even as Lozar was ducking away. They circled in the center of the store, knocking over a display of canned goods and scattering a rack of brooms leaning against the counter. Nettles ran around wildly, begging them to go outside. Lozar paid no attention to the store-keeper and Dusty didn't take his eyes off the gunman.

Seeing that he couldn't outbox Dusty, Lozar suddenly charged straight at him. Dusty had been anticipating that and agilely stepped aside, bringing his right hand around like a club, catching Lozar on the side of the jaw.

Lozar staggered past Dusty, caught himself on a counter, knocking everything off the top, then wheeled back. He rushed forward again, dodging just as he neared Dusty, hoping to come to grips with him. But Dusty stepped backward, catching Lozar with a punch in the nose that brought blood although it lacked the force of his first blow.

Before Lozar could swing around to come at Dusty again, Dusty had landed a heavy blow on the side of the gunman's head. Lozar staggered again, slamming into an open flour barrel from which Nettles had been doling out small amounts to his customers. Flour exploded into the air, settling over Lozar as he lost his footing and slid to the floor beside the barrel.

With a gutteral squall, Lozar came off the floor and Dusty saw the knife in his hand. He wasn't greatly surprised that Lozar would be prepared with some trick like that in case he couldn't win with his fists.

When Lozar charged this time, Dusty concentrated on keeping out of his way. His dodging brought him against another counter on which set a big rack of spices and seasonings. Flipping a glance at the rack, Dusty saw the box of black pepper. He grabbed it off the rack as he dodged away from Lozar.

Lozar came at Dusty slower now, confident that he'd catch up with him sooner or later. Dusty watched him carefully, staying on the balls of his feet. He gripped the pepper can in both hands and twisted, forcing the top off the can.

As Lozar charged at Dusty again, Dusty flung the can of pepper into his face. Lozar screamed and fell back, clawing at his eyes. In a moment he began sneezing, cursing loudly between sneezes.

He still clutched his knife but Dusty moved forward and grabbed his wirst, banging it across the top of the cracker barrel. The knife flipped away, sliding under the counter.

Lozar still tried to fight but he couldn't see anything and Dusty cracked him a sharp blow on the chin that took the fight out of him. Then he dragged him toward the door.

"Where are you taking me?" Lozar gasped between sneezes.

"To jail," Dusty said. "For attacking an officer."

"What about my store?" Nettles yelled, coming out on the porch. "You ruined my store."

"Lozar will pay for the damage," Dusty said. "He'll rot in jail till he does."

"I'll—I'll kill you for this!" Lozar gasped as Dusty dragged him up the sidewalk to the jail next door to the store.

Torberg jumped to his feet as Dusty shoved Lozar into the deputy's office. "What are you doing with him?" he demanded.

"Throwing him in jail," Dusty said and pushed Lozar into one of the three cells there and slammed the door.

"You can't use my jail," Torberg shouted.

"I've got to have some place to put my prisoners," Dusty said.

"This is a county jail."

"This is in the city limits of Jawbone," Dusty said. "I'm marshal here. I'll use your jail till the town council says I can't. You might give Lozar some water to wash the pepper out of his eyes."

He went outside with Torberg screaming after him. From the porch of the deputy's office, he saw Pettigrew standing in front of the bank motioning to him. He stepped off into the dust of the street and angled across to the bank.

"What's wrong?" Dusty demanded when he reached the bank. "Don't you approve of me arresting Ben Lozar?"

"I wouldn't care if you killed him," Pettigrew said.

41

"In fact, I wish you would. I called you over to tell you Craig Usta is in town."

Hunch hadn't followed Dusty to the jail but he had crossed the street from the store and was standing beside Dusty now.

"Am I suppose to cheer or run and hide?" Dusty asked.

Pettigrew scowled. "We hired you to make sure that Usta and his hired guns don't stop the settlers from building their dam. I just heard that Usta has called a meeting for this afternoon. I want you to break it up."

"There's nothing illegal in holding a meeting," Dusty said.

"They're planning something illegal, you can bet on that. Just break it up."

"I have no power outside town," Dusty reminded the banker.

"I hear this meeting is to be in the feed store. That's in town."

"When is it?"

"This afternoon some time. Find out what they're planning then stop it. And get a gun. You're going to have to have one."

IV

Dusty looked down the street after the banker had gone back inside. There were several horses racked in front of the saloon now and he guessed that was where Craig Usta was at the moment. He might hold his

42

meeting there, too. Calling a meeting at the feed store didn't make such sense to Dusty.

"What are you going to do about that?" Hunch asked.

"Very little till we find out what is going to happen," Dusty said. "Can't kill a snake till you find out which end his head is on."

"Look who's coming out of the saloon," Hunch said suddenly.

Dusty saw Zeke Torberg leading two other men through the swinging doors. One was a huge man that Dusty hadn't seen before. Somehow he was sure that was Craig Usta. Behind him came another smaller man. They walked the short distance to the deputy's office to the south of the saloon and disappeared inside.

"Come on, Hunch. We'd better see about this."

They crossed the street to the walk in front of the store and turned north toward the jail. As they stepped up on the porch of the deputy's office, the big man came out followed by the smaller man and Ben Lozar.

"How did he get out of jail?" Dusty demanded, jerking a thumb at Lozar.

"I told Torberg to let him out," the big man said. "You're the new marshal, I hear. I'm Craig Usta. You don't lock up one of my men on some silly charge."

"He was put there till he pays the damage done to Tom Nettles' store," Dusty said.

"I'll take care of that personally," Usta said.

Dusty sized up the big man. He was six feet three or

43

four inches tall and Dusty guessed him to weigh at least two hundred and twenty-five pounds. He had iron gray hair and yellowish-brown eyes that bored into Dusty now. Dusty guessed he was seldom crossed by anybody.

"Lozar was also in jail for attacking a law officer."

"There's only one law officer in this town—Zeke Torberg. And Ben didn't attack him. But if you want to try to make something of it, just let me know when the judge gets around to the county seat and I'll have Ben there."

Dusty knew he couldn't take Lozar from Craig Usta and put him back in jail. Not even if he had a gun. He'd have to wait for a better time to lock horns with the Big U owner.

"I want to see a receipt from Tom Nettles that the damage done to his store has been paid," Dusty said.

"I'll have it signed and delivered to Zeke's office here," Usta said. "You can gloat over it as long as you like."

Usta pushed past Dusty and Hunch and went down to the store, Lozar and the Big U rider going with him. Lozar threw some choice words at Dusty as he went past but Dusty ignored him.

"What now?" Hunch asked.

"We've got to find out about that meeting. Let's see what Fred Yoeman knows."

They crossed the street again to the hardware store. Yoeman and a fanner were inside watching the action across the street. Dusty sized up the farmer. He was dressed like Ed Klosson but he was much smaller with black hair and dark murky eyes.

"Dusty Dekin, this is Orlo Quill," Yoeman introduced. "Orlo has a place a couple of miles above Klosson's."

"Glad to meet you, Dekin," Quill said. "My place is just below the site where our dam will be put in."

Dusty shook hands with Quill then introduced Hunch. "We've been hearing about a meeting Usta has called for this afternoon. Know anything about it?"

Quill shook his head. "If he's calling a meeting, it's probably to plan how to burn us settlers out."

"That's just a guess, isn't it?" Dusty asked.

"Usta told us when we first settled on the river that he'd burn us out if we didn't leave," Quill said.

"But he hasn't done it."

"He will," Quill insisted. "Usta wants that river grass for his winter feed. He's let us alone because there are only a few of us. But now that we're planning to build a dam and bring in more farmers, he's going on the war path. He won't stop at anything."

"He's right, Dusty," Yoeman said. "If we put in that dam, settlers will swarm in here like flies and Usta knows he won't have any grass left to cut."

"You've got to show Usta he can't run the whole country," Quill said.

"He doesn't strike me as a man who can be shown anything," Dusty said.

He went outside followed by Hunch. Most of the horses were gone from the front of Gumpy's Saloon and Dusty saw Usta and some riders reining in at the livery barn down by the river.

"Let's see what they'll tell us at the saloon," Dusty said.

In the saloon, they were virtually ignored. Dusty decided that Gumpy catered strictly to Usta and the ranchers. He and Hunch said nothing but Dusty listened intently to every word said around him. He heard the meeting mentioned and he knew that Pettigrew had his information straight. It was to be in the feed store according to one puncher still standing at the bar drinking. Dusty guessed that there was some doubt in Usta's mind that all those in the saloon should hear what was going to be said at that meeting.

Vyrl Wolfe came in and looked around the darkened interior until he saw Dusty and Hunch. Coming over to them quickly, he tugged at Dusty's sleeve.

"I'd like to see you in my office, Dusty."

Dusty nodded. He and Hunch followed the engineer out into the street and around to the side door of the bank.

"Phoebus was telling me about the meeting Usta has called," Wolfe said. "I'm betting he's planning to wreck my construction camp. That would stop all the work on the dam."

Dusty nodded. This made more sense than Quill's prediction that Usta's men were going to burn out the settlers.

"What do you expect me to do about it?" Dusty asked. "Your camp is outside of town."

"Their meeting isn't," Wolfe said. "If you can break up that meeting before they can map out any plans, it will delay things, at least."

Dusty nodded. "I reckon it would. Whatever they're planning, they must aim to keep it a secret or they wouldn't hold their meeting in the feed store where nobody can overhear them."

"I'll appreciate anything you can do," Wolfe said.

"Any idea why Usta is holding that meeting here in town instead of out at his ranch?"

Wolfe nodded. "Probably because he wants Torberg and Lozar in on it. Torberg stays pretty close to town and Lozar is always here, even though he works for Usta."

"How many will be at that meeting?" Dusty asked.

"Hard to say," Wolfe said. "You might check the number of Big U horses down at the livery barn. Most of the tough hands the ranchers have hired stay at the Big U. Lozar rides a Big U horse, too. Add Torberg to the number of Big U horses you find and you'll know about how many men you'll have to buck at that meeting. They'll all be top hands with a gun."

Dusty and Hunch went outside. Usta was just leading some men back into the saloon. Dusty decided this was a good time to check the barn. They headed south across the side street then angled over to the barn.

Dusty ignored the liveryman when he asked what they wanted. Walking down the long alleyway behind the horses, he read the brands in the dim light. He

47

counted six Big U horses. Adding Torberg, that would mean at least seven men at the meeting.

"I'm not hankering to tackle that many gun slicks at once," Hunch said.

"Me, either," Dusty agreed. "But Wolfe is probably guessing right on what the meeting is about. We could buy a little time if we could break it up. Time is what we need to find the men you and I are looking for."

At the end of the barn runway, they were stopped by a donkey that ambled in from the corral.

"What's a donkey doing here?" Hunch demanded.

"That's old Golddust," the liveryman said, coming up behind them. "We've had him here for a year. Can't get nobody to take him off our hands."

"You don't rent him out much, I take it," Hunch said.

"Don't never rent him out," the liveryman said. "He's a deadbeat. An old prospector led this donkey all the way from the mountains where he'd been panning for gold. Hadn't even found enough dust to pay for stage fare back east. He talked me into taking his old donkey in exchange for enough money to ride home on. Sure played me for a sucker."

"Maybe you should go prospecting," Dusty said, his mind more on the meeting coming up than on the donkey.

"Wouldn't trust that donkey as far as I could see a freckle on his nose," the man retorted. "The prospector said he was perfectly reliable unless he smelled a bear. Seems he had a tangle with a bear up in the hills once and he goes crazy whenever he smells one."

"He's not liable to smell one here," Hunch said.

Dusty and Hunch started back toward the main part of town. They heard some furious barking as they passed the feed store and Dusty saw Jennie's little dog, Napoleon, at one corner of the feed store.

"Better leave that critter alone," Hunch advised when Dusty paused.

Dusty sniffed the air. "He must have located a skunk den. Maybe we'd better rescue him before he really gets stunk up."

"Good place for skunks," Hunch said, "under the building where the polecats are going to meet to plot against the dam builders."

Dusty shouted at the dog and he tucked his tail between his legs and headed toward the boarding house. Dusty and Hunch followed him.

Dusty saw that school was out for the day and the children were rushing away from the building or getting their horses to ride home. By the time Dusty and Hunch had reached the boarding house, Jennie had appeared in front of the school house to pound the dust out of some erasers against the side of the building. The little dog saw her and dashed across the street to her from the boarding house.

Before Dusty could get inside the boarding house, he was hailed from across the street.

"Are you responsible for my dog getting in a fight with a skunk?" Jennie demanded, running across toward them.

49

Dusty frowned. "I suppose you think I looked up a skunk den and shoved your dog into it."

"I wouldn't put it past you after the way you treated Napoleon at noon," she snapped. "I saw you follow Napoleon up from the feed store."

Dusty shook his head. Jennie Blair wanted to think the worst of him and there wasn't anything he could do about it. She was the prettiest girl he had ever seen. He wondered if she was as pretty when she wasn't mad; he'd never seen her any other way. She was over a foot shorter than he was and wouldn't weigh more than a hundred pounds, soaking wet. But she had enough spunk to make up for any lack of size.

"If your dog is going to play with skunks, he's got to expect to smell like one."

"The same way with gunmen," Jennie snapped and spun on her heel and went back to the school house.

"Her temper is twice as big as she is," Hunch said softly.

"But she is pretty!" Dusty said. "I can see why Torberg hangs around her. Wonder if she tears into him like that."

"Bet there ain't a man alive big enough to handle her," Hunch said.

"You'd better believe that," Molly said from the doorway behind them.

Dusty wheeled. "Didn't hear you come out," he said. "Do you always slip up on people like that?"

Molly snorted. "I slip around about as quiet as a hippopotamus." She grinned. "Of course, I do manage to

50

hear things sometimes that aren't meant for my ears."

"Maybe you've heard what Usta's meeting is all about," Dusty said.

"Well now," Molly said, eyes twinkling, "Ben Lozar was just here after some more ammunition for his gun. Seems somebody borrowed his gun and when he got it back, it was empty. He said something about planning real trouble for some dam builders."

Dusty nodded. "Sort of figured that. Know who will be at that meeting?"

"You're pretty nosey, aren't you?"

"I sure am," Dusty said. "Sometimes being nosey keeps a fellow from walking into a hornet's nest."

Molly nodded thoughtfully. "I'd say Craig Usta will probably have most of the gunmen the ranchers have brought in plus the deputy sheriff and of course, Ben Lozar. Since Tom Nettles has the only safe in town except the one in the bank, I reckon he'll be invited. He won't like it but he'll be too scared to stay away. Usta is going to make Nettles keep the money the ranchers are borrowing to pay their hired guns, I hear."

Hunch nudged Dusty. "Looks like they're starting to gather at the feed store now."

Dusty turned to look across the vacant lots at the feed store south of the bank. Four men were walking toward the store. One of them was Usta.

"I've got to start supper," Molly said. "If you're planning on walking into that feed store to break up that meeting, I won't bother to put on anything for you."

"I figure on eating here tonight, Molly," Dusty said. "Don't even plan on being late."

Molly went back inside and Dusty turned his attention to the men moving toward the feed store. He was sure he recognized Zeke Torberg and Tom Nettles among the men going inside.

Then his attention was caught by Jennie leaving the school house and coming across toward the boarding house, her little dog frisking along beside her.

"Are you good at making friends with dogs?" Dusty asked softly.

"Never had a dog bite me," Hunch said. "What's stewing in your mind now?"

"I'll tell you after we get that dog. Now I'm going to talk to Jennie and I want you to get Napoleon. Don't let him make a sound. I'll meet you behind the bank."

Hunch started to object but Dusty moved away to meet Jennie. As he approached her, he tipped his hat and smiled. She hesitated, watching him suspiciously.

"I'm sorry that I got off on the wrong foot with you, Miss Blair," Dusty said. "I hope we can be friends."

She looked at him sharply, suspicion hedging her words. "I'd rather be friends than enemies with a dog."

He winced. "Knowing how you like dogs, I'm taking that as a compliment. Is there anything I can do to make amends?"

The suspicion deepened in her eyes. "Not unless you want to help with the last day of school program."

Dusty grinned. "I'm not much good at giving recitations. When's this program coming up?"

52

"Day after tomorrow. It's going to be a big day for the children. I hope nothing happens to ruin it."

Dusty knew she was thinking of the explosive situation between the ranchers and the settlers and he had to admit she had good reason to be worried. He glanced around. Hunch was out of sight and the dog was just disappearing around the corner of the boarding house. Hunch had some kind of magic that attracted dogs.

"I'll do what I can to keep the lid on things," Dusty said. "If there is anything I can do to help you with that program, just call on me."

He turned and headed slowly toward the main part of town. Jennie watched him go, a puzzled look on her face. She was just as pretty when she wasn't mad, he decided. She was so small, she looked like a school girl herself. The plan he had for using Napoleon suddenly became a sour taste in his mouth. But he had to put business ahead of his own satisfaction.

When he reached the bank, he turned to look for Hunch. As he had expected, Jennie had gone inside the boarding house when he left. Now Hunch was coming from the back of the boarding house with the dog under his arm.

"How did he behave?" Dusty asked when Hunch reached him.

"Like a charm," Hunch said. "He's used to being carried. Most dogs wouldn't put up with this. What's on your mind?"

"Remember how that dog loves to go after skunks?"

53

Hunch nodded. "That school teacher blamed us for shoving him in with the skunks."

"This time we really *will* push him in with them."

Hunch grinned. Then his grin broke into a chuckle. "Mix one dog with that nest of skunks under the feed store and there'll be no meeting in that building."

"Exactly," Dusty said. "But I do hate to get that dog stunk up."

"Yeah," Hunch agreed, still chuckling. "That teacher will shoot you on sight when her dog gets back."

Dusty sighed. "A bath and a good airing will eventually fix up the dog. But what those fellows in that feed store are planning can't be fixed up that easy. Let's go."

V

When Dusty and Hunch arrived at the north side of the feed store, which had no windows, Dusty could hear men's voices inside, but he couldn't understand what was being said. He glanced back toward town. He hoped no one saw Hunch and him here but if they did, it couldn't be helped. Napoleon was whining and squirming in Hunch's arms.

"He smells them," Hunch whispered.

"He's not alone. They surely must get a whiff of that perfume inside, too."

"Shall I let this dog down?"

Dusty nodded. "Let's see if he wants to go after those skunks again."

54

Hunch set Napoleon down, and the little dog leaped to the edge of the building immediately and began sniffing. Then he set to work clawing at the dirt around the hole, trying to make it big enough for him to crawl in.

Dusty found a sharp stick and, pushing the dog back, clawed the dirt away. Within a minute, he had a good sized hole opened up. It seemed to him that the odor was getting stronger.

"Suppose we're getting them worked up already?" Hunch asked.

"Maybe. When we see that dog go under the building, we'd better make tracks for other places."

Hunch let Napoleon loose again and the little dog dived at the hole. He disappeared into it like a frightened ground squirrel. The building was sitting on two-by-twelve floor joists so there was plenty of room for the dog to move around once he got through the dirt that had been banked up around the base of the building to keep the wind from blowing under it.

Dusty nodded at Hunch and they walked as rapidly as possible back to the bank building and around the corner where they could be hidden but still see the result of Napoleon's invasion of the skunk den.

Even from the bank, they could hear Napoleon growling and yapping. But suddenly those yaps turned to excited, terrified yips. A moment later Napoleon exploded out of the hole, scattering dirt and dust in every direction. A short distance from the building, he stopped to paw at his eyes than rub his head in the dirt.

"He must have got a direct hit," Hunch said softly.

"If there was that much perfume released under that feed store, it ought to have some effect on the meeting pretty soon."

As if in response to Dusty's prediction, the door of the feed store burst open and men poured out, pushing and swearing. They charged away from the door as if they couldn't move fast enough. Most went toward the livery barn to get their horses. Their curses aimed at the skunks and the dog that had roused them could have been heard all over town.

"I reckon that's the end of that meeting," Dusty said.

Hunch sighed happily. "That's sure a safer way of breaking it up than wading in with guns."

Dusty nodded. "All it cost is one sick dog. That may not seem like much to us but I know a certain lady who is going to disagree."

Hunch held up one hand solemnly. "Word of honor. I didn't see any dog tangle with any skunks."

Dusty grinned. "Some things you don't have to see. We'd better catch Napoleon and give him a bath."

"Second hand essence of skunk doesn't appeal to me," Hunch said. "Reckon that's better, though, than getting it first hand. Why don't we just let him take his own bath?"

"He might decide to go back to the boarding house for that bath," Dusty said.

"Looks to me like he's heading for the saloon. Suppose he thinks he needs a drink?"

"If he'd swallow a brick now, he couldn't keep it down. Let's go."

They left the bank and angled across the street in the wake of the dog. Hunch had guessed right. The dog did go directly to the saloon and slipped under the swinging doors. Dusty and Hunch were not far behind him.

At the door of the saloon, however, they were almost flattened by three men banging through the doors and out into the street, one of them holding his nose. Two of the men who had been at the meeting were on their horses now heading north out of town in the direction of Usta's Big U ranch.

"At least, that dog can't hide from us," Hunch said softly. "As long as we can smell we could find him under a ton of dirt."

Inside the saloon, Dusty saw the last of the customers disappearing out the hack door. The bartender was only a step behind, pushing them in his eagerness to get outside.

Napoleon had barely paused in the saloon. He was following the men out the back door, which they had left open in their haste to clear the room. Dusty was following them but he suddenly stopped as he was passing the bar. He caught Hunch's sleeve.

"Look here!" he exclaimed. "Looks like Pa's watch."

Quickly he picked up the watch some man had left on the bar. Turning it over, he saw the inscription on the back, dim with wear but still readable. "To Matt Dekin from the town of Abilene."

"This is Pa's watch, all right. But who left it here?"

"Could have been anyone in here," Hunch said. "Reckon he must have been checking the time when Napoleon came in. Everybody left in sort of a hurry."

"We've got to find out who was in here," Dusty said.

"Going to take the watch?"

Dusty shook his head. "Whoever claims this watch now would know then that we're on his trail. Don't want to let that happen. But we've *got* to find out who was in here when that dog scared them out."

Laying the watch back on the bar, Dusty headed through the back door. He had proof now that Charley Davis had been right. The man who had murdered his father was surely in Jawbone. And that man knew that Dusty was Matt Dekin's son. If he suspected that Dusty was looking for him, he'd make sure Dusty never lived to find out who he was.

Napoleon was nowhere in sight when they reached the alley. Some of the men who had dashed out the back door were returning rather cautiously. Gumpy Alvis, who owned the saloon, and Serg Sitzman, the gambler, were among the men. Dusty didn't recognize any of the others. He realized that there had been several men in the saloon. It was going to be hard to find out which one claimed that watch.

"Follow the dog," he said to Hunch. "I'm going back in and see who picks up that watch."

Dusty turned and followed the men inside the saloon. The minute he was through the back door, his eyes raked the bar. But the watch was gone. Three

58

men were standing there demanding a drink to wash out the smell. Gumpy was serving as bartender and Sitzman had already dropped in a chair with a deck of cards in his hand.

Dusty looked sharply at the three men at the bar. One was a settler and the other two looked like cowboys. None of them had the appearance of a man capable of murder. Then Dusty discovered that a couple of other men had come in the front door, probably while the others were still out behind. But they were settlers, too, and fell far short of filling the picture Dusty had of his father's killer.

He thought of asking the men for the time of day. But the man he was looking for was in this room and that question might tip him off that Dusty was on his trail. There had to be a safer, surer way of finding out who claimed that watch.

Ducking back out the rear door, Dusty went after Hunch. He found the hunchback across the street, moving along beside the hardware store.

"Where did the dog go?" Dusty asked when he caught up.

"Home," Hunch said. "I wouldn't recommend going to the boarding house until that school teacher has time to cool down."

"We'll miss our supper if we do that," Dusty said.

"You may be missing your front teeth if you don't," Hunch predicted.

"We'll keep our mouths shut," Dusty said. "That will protect our teeth."

At the boarding house Molly was letting the world know how she felt about having a polecat's cousin just outside the back door. Jennie was outside with a tub of water and some soap trying to coax Napoleon into the tub. The little dog had discovered that everybody either avoided him or tried to kick him and his faith in the human race was badly shaken.

"Did that dog go back to the skunks?" Dusty asked innocently.

"Somebody took him back," Jennie said angrily, looking at Dusty suspiciously. "He wouldn't go near a skunk unless he was encouraged."

"He was doing all right by himself when I chased him away from that skunk den earlier this afternoon," Dusty said. "Need some help giving him a bath?"

"If you want to help," Jennie said. "Somehow I have the feeling you've got a guilty conscience."

Dusty held up a hand. "Wouldn't touch such a thing."

Jennie called the dog and when he came creeping toward her, Dusty caught him and doused him into the tub where Jennie began scrubbing him with soap and a brush. Molly came out to watch the procedure.

"Had a man here a couple of minutes ago who could have used a bath like that," she said.

"Who was that?" Dusty asked quickly.

"Craig Usta. He smelled so strong, I looked for the stripe down his back. He wanted to see Ben Lozar. Ben smelled some himself but not as bad as Usta."

"Now what do you suppose Usta wanted to see Lozar about?" Dusty mused.

"Well, if you ask me," Molly said, "I'd guess the ranchers are planning on holding up the stage that's bringing in the money to pay for the dam. They'll do anything to stop that dam and stealing the money would do it."

Dusty had been thinking in terms of what the ranchers might do to Vyrl Wolfe's construction camp or to the homesteads of the settlers. But what Molly suggested made sense, too. Stealing the money would be the easiest way of wrecking the settlers' plans and it carried the least risk of detection.

"Think you can handle Napoleon by yourself?" he said to Jennie. "I've got to see a man."

"I can handle him," Jennie said. "Maybe you can find another skunk den for Napoleon to raid."

Dusty sighed. Jennie was still angry. She wasn't sure that Dusty was guilty but she was very suspicious. If anybody in Jawbone was on Jennie's black list, Dusty was the one.

Dusty headed toward the bank, Hunch keeping step with him. Banking hours were over for the day but Pettigrew might still be there. They found him just locking the front door.

"Molly thinks the ranchers might try to rob the stage bringing in the money for the dam," Dusty said.

"I've thought of that," Pettigrew said worriedly. "That stage comes in tomorrow morning shortly after sun-up. If they robbed that stage, they'd not only stop the dam building but they'd have plenty of money to pay their gun slingers. Dusty, I want you to kill Ben

61

Lozar. That would put a crimp in their plans."

"That would also put a crimp in my life line," Dusty said. "Lozar would like nothing better than to have me face him with a gun."

"Accommodate him," Pettigrew said.

"I don't kill people, Mr. Pettigrew," Dusty said. "I have never fired a gun at a man in my life."

"They told me you stopped that whole passel of Big U riders out south of town with a sawed-off shotgun."

"I didn't fire that gun," Dusty said. "They just didn't know I wouldn't shoot."

"Well, if that don't salt the beans!" Pettigrew snorted. "Maybe you should turn in your badge."

"Your town council gave me this badge on a unanimous vote," Dusty said. "I'll see what I can do about stopping that hold-up."

Pettigrew stared at Dusty, then nodded across the street. "There goes our fearless deputy sheriff now."

"Where do you figure he's going?"

"I'd guess out to Craig Usta's ranch," Pettigrew said. "Usta and his men left a few minutes ago. They probably figure they won't be interrupted if they continue their meeting out at the ranch tonight."

"Be nice to know just what they are planning," Hunch said softly.

"I was thinking the same thing," Dusty agreed. "Maybe we'd ought to see what Usta's ranch looks like."

"They may not have any skunks out there," Pettigrew said and started up the street toward his big house at the north end of town.

"Guess we had to expect Pettigrew to see us send that dog into the skunks den," Dusty said. "There's no building between the bank and the feed store. Let's see if Lozar has headed for the Big U, too."

They retraced their steps to the boarding house. Jennie had finished with the dog's bath and Napoleon was standing at the corner of the house shaking himself vigorously, trying to get all the water off his fur.

Dusty went inside where Molly was in the kitchen getting supper ready. "Is Ben Lozar here now?" he asked.

"No," Molly said disgustedly. "He rode out a few minutes ago, heading north. Waited until I had supper on to cook before he told me he wouldn't be here."

"Better not figure on Hunch and me for supper, either," Dusty said.

"You scalawags!" Molly screamed. "Let me cook up enough for a threshing crew then you run out. Afraid of my cooking?"

"We're just afraid we'll miss something more important than supper," Dusty said. "Sorry, Molly. We'll eat twice as much for breakfast."

"Like fun you will!" Molly snorted. "You'll get just the same amount as you would if you stayed here and ate supper like civilized human beings."

Dusty and Hunch went to the livery stable and got their horses. They rode east along the river until they were out of sight of the town then swung north and circled back to the road leading north from the town to Craig Usta's ranch.

Usta's Big U ranch was five miles from town and it was almost dark by the time Dusty and Hunch arrived. Dusty reined up well south of the buildings and sat there looking over the yard. Light streamed from a window in the front of the house, revealing a couple of horses hitched to the rack in front. There was a light in the bunkhouse but no other sign of life was visible.

"Suppose they'll have a guard out?" Hunch asked.

"It's possible," Dusty admitted. "They probably don't trust the settlers much farther than the settlers trust them. Looks like an empty corral on this side of the barn. Maybe we can tie our horses there and slip up to the house."

They left their horses tied to the top rail of the corral fence then moved silently toward the house. It was full dark now and if there was a guard stationed outside the house, he was well hidden. Dusty and Hunch reached the house without a challenge and slid along the wall until they were near the window.

The window was closed but shortly after they reached it, a man came over and slid it up a few inches, saying it was getting hot inside with so many men in the room.

Through the half open window, Dusty could hear and see what was going on. Usta was standing at a table with Zeke Torberg beside him. Ben Lozar was only a short distance away. Dusty didn't know the other men.

"It's agreed then," Usta was saying, "that we'll hit the stage at the bluffs west of town just after it comes out of the ford. Ben, it will be your job to take care of the driver."

"That will be easy," Lozar said. "The sun will be in his eyes. I'll hide behind Hat Rock. That will keep me in the shadow and give me a good shot."

"We'll split up right at the site," Usta said. "Nobody can trail us. They'll suspect who did it but they can't prove it. With no money, the dam project will stop."

"We're going to have to get up pretty early," Torberg said. "We should be in position shortly after the sun comes up. I'm heading for the sack."

Dusty nudged Hunch and they ran toward the corral, keeping low so they wouldn't be seen. They were just passing the well in the center of the yard when Hunch tripped over a stick and fell.

"Hold it!" someone hissed over by the door of the house. "Thought I heard something."

VI

Dusty dropped down behind the winch of the well and held his breath. Hunch lay right where he had fallen. Flat on the ground, he was invisible from the house.

There was silence at the house and silence over the yard. Finally one man at the house broke it.

"You must have been hearing things, Zeke. Everything is as quiet as a graveyard."

"I reckon so," Zeke Torberg said. "I sure don't want anybody knowing I'm in on this scheme."

"Usta is paying you a lot better than that deputy

badge does," one man reminded him.

Two men mounted the horses and rode out of the yard while the rest went on to the bunkhouse. Dusty didn't move till they had all disappeared. There wasn't much light but the two saddled horses could have been seen at the corner of the empty corral if anyone had looked.

But no one did look and Dusty and Hunch hurried on to the horses after the yard had emptied of its visitors. They rode at a slow pace back to town, again circling to the east so that they came into town from the direction they had gone out.

The saloon was still open. Dusty and Hunch tied their horses at the bank and walked across the street to the saloon. They found it almost empty.

Serg Sitzman, the gambler, was sitting at a table, idly shuffling the cards. He saw Dusty and Hunch and called them over.

"Want to play a hand or two?" he invited.

"Pretty tired," Dusty said. "Just thought we'd look in and see who was here."

"Nobody's here now," Sitzman said. "But Torberg and Ben Lozar just left. Looked to me like they'd been riding. Sort of late at night for that, don't you think?"

Dusty nodded. "Reckon it is. But that's their business."

"Since you're the marshal, I thought you might be interested," Sitzman said.

"My jurisdiction doesn't extend beyond the town limits," Dusty reminded him. "Thanks for the interest, though. It's not like Lozar to ride around without good reason. Got any idea what that reason might be?"

"Maybe he's looking for a way to kill you," Sitzman said. "Or he could be planning to steal the settlers' money."

"Or maybe both," Dusty added thoughtfully. "Thanks for the tip."

When Dusty and Hunch were outside, Hunch snorted. "He didn't tell you anything you didn't already know."

"Not about Lozar," Dusty said. "But he told me something about himself. He's trying to be unusually helpful and he doesn't strike me as a man who makes a habit of being helpful. Maybe he wants me to nose into Lozar's business so that either Lozar or me gets killed. I'd like to know which one he wants dead."

Hunch sighed. "I reckon we're going to nose in without any urging from Sitzman. What do you figure on doing?"

"Sleep on it," Dusty said. "But we'll have to sleep fast. That stage gets to the hold-up site just after sun-up. We've got to be there first."

Dusty and Hunch picketed the horses in some good grass west of town not far from the boarding house. They didn't want to notify the town they were leaving early the next morning by going to the livery barn for their horses.

At the boarding house, they were surprised to find Molly still up, keeping some food warm on the stove.

"I don't like hungry people sleeping in my beds,"

Molly grumbled when Dusty thanked her for the supper.

"How about Ben Lozar? Did you keep his supper warm, too?"

Molly frowned. "How did you know he wasn't here? He hasn't come in yet. I figure he's staying with somebody else tonight."

"Glad to hear it," Dusty said. "We have to leave early in the morning. Wouldn't want to wake him up."

Dusty and Hunch were well up the river before sun-up the next morning. Molly had explained that the best place for the stage to cross the river between Pronghorn and Jawbone was three miles above the town and that explained why the stage road came into Jawbone from the west.

The first rays of sunlight revealed the crossing and the rocky bluffs on the north side of the river just to the east of the ford. Dusty scrutinized the area. He saw no horses or men. Apparently he and Hunch had arrived ahead of Usta's men.

"There's the Hat Rock Lozar mentioned," Dusty said, pointing out a rock spire with a flat top like an umbrella a hundred yards east of the ford.

Carefully searching the bluffs close to the river, Dusty picked out a spot to hide where he and Hunch couldn't be seen from either the ford or the hiding place Lozar had chosen. Dusty rode upstream beyond the ford and dismounted, ground hitching his horse where he was out of sight of anyone downstream. Hunch did the same.

Back at his selected site, Dusty took a square piece

of glass he had removed from the mirror in his room at Molly's boarding house. Holding it in the early rays of the sun, he concentrated the sun's reflection on various spots until he was satisfied that he could control it.

"You'll warn anybody within a mile that we're here," Hunch said.

"Only if they are straight down the river," Dusty said. "I don't figure Usta's men are going to ride up the river bottom. They're the only ones who should be out this early. Now all we can do is wait and hope everything works out as we have it planned."

"Don't forget they've done some planning, too," Hunch said dubiously.

"I hope they stick to their plans," Dusty said. "If they don't, our scheme won't work."

Within five minutes several riders came over the bluffs from the northeast. Dusty and Hunch watched them from their place of concealment. One man took the horses back beyond the bluffs to the north. The others settled into hidden places among the rocks. One man came on to the wide-capped rock and squatted down in its shadow.

Less than five minutes later, the stage appeared from the south, bearing down on the ford. Dusty checked the angle of the sun. The driver of the stage was going to be looking almost directly into it when he came out of the ford and headed the team toward Jawbone. But it also gave Dusty a perfect angle for his reflection from the mirror.

The coach splashed across the river and wheeled to the east. Dusty, watching Lozar, saw him ease up to one knee, his rifle over that knee. Dusty slipped out of his hiding place and brought his mirror around into the sun.

For a second, the reflection flashed against the rocks. Then it concentrated on Lozar's face, flashing a brilliant light into his eyes. Lozar squeezed off his shot but he was flinching from the glare in his eyes and the bullet split the air well above the coach.

The stage driver dropped out of sight behind the dash and yelled at his team. Dusty kept his light flashing at Lozar as the gunman tried to jack another cartridge into the rifle and aim again. He stood up, brushing his hand before his eyes. The guard on the coach snapped a shot at him and missed but it came close enough to make Lozar dodge back. He lost his footing and fell a dozen feet down the slope to lodge against some rocks.

Dusty wondered whether the others would open fire but they apparently were too surprised at what had happened to react quickly enough and their moment was gone.

"Bring the horses!" one man yelled.

"We'd better get our horses," Dusty said and sprinted to the west where their horses were standing. He had the reins of both horses by the time Hunch arrived. In a moment, they were in the saddle and kicking their horses into a run.

They hit the road a hundred yards behind Usta's

men. The stage coach was another three hundred yards ahead. Dusty urged his horse to his top speed. He soon cut the distance between him and the Big U riders by half. Then one of the men saw Dusty and Hunch and called Usta's attention to them.

Dusty wondered if they'd begin shooting at him and Hunch but instead, Usta and his men reined up until the two could catch up.

"What are you doing here?" Usta demanded.

Dusty reined his horse down to a pace matching the Big U riders. "We heard some shooting and rushed over to see if we were needed. I can see that we aren't. Sure glad to know there are some law-abiding citizens around to help make sure the stage isn't held up."

Usta and Torberg exchanged glances and Torberg nodded. "I'd heard that there might be some trouble waiting for this stage. That's why we came out. Good thing we did."

"Sure is," Dusty agreed. "Well, we can all escort it into town. Won't be any trouble with this many of us to watch it."

Dusty looked over the men and noticed that Ben Lozar was not among the riders. Maybe he had been hurt in his fall. Ahead, the coach slowed down from its breakneck speed as the driver saw that the riders had eased their pace.

They went into town that way, the stage a quarter of a mile ahead of the riders. By the time Dusty and the others arrived, the passengers were unloaded and most of the baggage had been taken from the boot.

"Hey, Torberg," the driver yelled as soon as he recognized the deputy, "Where were you? We were almost held up out there."

Torberg nodded. "I'd heard that there was something afoot. That's why I was out there with a posse. You don't think that hold-up man would have stopped with one shot if we hadn't been there, do you?"

"I don't know what to think," the driver said. "First that rifleman takes a shot at us and misses then he falls down the slope. Next thing we know a dozen riders are chasing us like a passel of Indians. Then they quit chasing us and trail us into town like a soldier escort."

"We were only trying to get close enough to you to make sure we could help you if those robbers tried anything else," Torberg said.

Dusty winked at Hunch and dismounted. The stage stop in Jawbone was at the grocery store since there was no hotel. Dusty guessed that the store had drawn the honor of being the stage station because, until Pettigrew started the bank, it had had the only safe in town where any valuables could be stored.

Tom Nettles was talking to the passengers who had gotten off the coach. Only one of them seemed to be staying, judging from the amount of baggage at her feet. She was a black haired woman and Dusty guessed her to be under thirty. Her black eyes flashed around, sizing up everything they contacted.

Nettles bustled around with a sheepish look as though he were apologizing for being alive but Dusty had decided that was his natural appearance. Phoebus

72

Pettigrew and one of his clerks were waiting at the boot for the money box. Pettigrew looked as nervous as a mouse trapped in a flour barrel, watching Usta and his men as if he expected them to pounce on him any second and take the money.

The woman with the baggage stepped over to Dusty, apparently attracted by his marshal's badge. "I'm Queeny Renick," she said, holding out her hand like a man. "Thought I'd stay a while and maybe sing at the saloon. This town looks like it could use some good entertainment."

Dusty nodded, taking her hand. "Most towns can stand that," he said. "How come you picked Jawbone?"

She smiled at him. "Maybe I heard Jawbone had a good looking marshal."

Dusty shook his head. "You'll have to do better than that."

"I don't have to do anything, Marshal," Queeny said. "Just remember that in case you get any ideas."

Pettigrew snatched at Dusty's arm then. "Help us get this money into the bank," he demanded. "You're going to have to guard it."

Dusty saw him glance at Queeny Renick and he was sure he heard him gasp but it was quickly stifled until he wondered if he had imagined it. Maybe the banker had drawn the same conclusion about Queeny that he had.

Dusty followed the clerk and Pettigrew to the bank. No one was going to take the money on this busy street but Pettigrew didn't seem to believe that.

"You're going to have to stay here and guard this," Pettigrew said.

"Hold on," Dusty objected. "I'm supposed to be marshal of the town, not just this bank. Anyway, nobody is going to get into your safe to get that money."

"Didn't they try to steal it out on the trail this morning?"

"Sure. But it didn't work. They won't be so bold here in town. Didn't you see who was escorting the stage in to make sure the money got here safely?"

"Safe, my eye!" Pettigrew snorted. "I don't know how you worked it to make it look like they were escorting the stage instead of trying to hold it up, but you can't always beat them by trickery."

"Who said anything about trickery?" Dusty asked. "We just caught up with them and we all rode into town together. Now you wouldn't expect them to admit they were trying to rob the stage, would you?"

"Everybody knows what they were up to!"

"Knowing it and proving it can be two different breeds of cats. I'll keep an eye on the bank."

Dusty went outside and Hunch shadowed him across to the saloon which was open in spite of the early hour. Serg Sitzman was standing at the window looking out.

"Looks like you've had a dusty ride this morning," he said.

"We were helping Torberg and Usta prevent a stage hold-up," Dusty said.

Sitzman nodded, a grin spreading over his face. "I'm sure they appreciated the help. Ben Lozar was bragging about getting a big cut of the money on that stage. He didn't know anybody but Torberg and Usta heard him."

"I'm afraid his cut will be a little smaller than he expected," Dusty said.

Sitzman puzzled him. The gambler seemed to be trying to be friendly. Dusty wondered if he was being too cautious where Sitzman was concerned. The gambler was in a position to tell him a lot that he might not be able to learn in other ways. And there were many things that Dusty needed to know.

The doors swung open and Dusty wheeled, expecting to see Craig Usta banging into the saloon. But it was the new resident of Jawbone, Queeny Renick. She stood with her hands on her hips, looking over everything and everybody in the place. Then she came straight to Sitzman.

"I figure on singing here in your place," she said. "I want a ten percent cut of your profits."

Sitzman scowled. "Hold on, lady. In the first place, I only work here. You'll have to see Gumpy; he owns the place. Besides, it ain't likely anybody is going to dish out ten percent of the profits just so you can warble a little."

"Look, buster," Queeny said. "When I sing, I draw in the crowds. You'll make twice as much as you're making now. That ten percent will be the best investment this place ever made." She ran her eyes over

Sitzman. "You sure look like the boss to me."

She went on to the bar where Sitzman had pointed out Gumpy Alvis. Before she reached him, Ben Lozar came in the door. His face was clawed up and his shirt was torn.

"What bear did you tangle with?" Sitzman asked, grinning.

"Shut up," Lozar snapped. "I was hunting and the rifle kicked. Knocked me over a bluff. I got scratched up."

Sitzman laughed. "That's a good story. You've been bragging about how good you are with a gun but you let a rifle kick you over a bluff."

"You shut up," Lozar repeated, dropping into a crouch, "or I'll show you how good I am with a gun."

The laughter faded from the gambler's voice and he held up a hand. "Don't get riled. I'm not questioning how good you are with a gun."

Dusty wasn't sure what might have developed if Craig Usta and a couple of his men hadn't come in then. Lozar turned to them and Usta led him off to a table at the far side of the saloon.

"Let's play a hand," Sitzman suggested to Dusty. "Over there." He indicated a table not too far from the one Usta had chosen.

Dusty nodded, knowing what Sitzman had in mind. Sitzman picked up his cards and they walked over to the table, Hunch taking a seat between Dusty and the gambler. Sitzman shuffled the cards quietly. Dusty didn't look at Usta's table but he was aware that the rancher had glared over at them then turned his attention back to Lozar who was still furious.

"I want my money," Lozar snapped.

"Keep your voice down," Usta said. "You didn't do your job."

Dusty had to strain his ears to hear. He picked up the cards Sitzman was dealing him but he paid no attention to them.

"It wasn't my fault," Lozar said in a softer voice. "I was blinded."

"That's likely!" Usta said sarcastically. "Anyway, since you loused up your job, there isn't any money to pay you until that buckboard gets here this afternoon. I'll see what I can do then."

"I get paid for my work, one way or another," Lozar said.

"You'll get paid," Usta said angrily. "But you've got a lot more work to do. Don't forget that."

Dusty, still looking at his cards, caught a glimpse out of the tail of his eye of Lozar glaring around the room, especially at him.

"It's going to be a pleasure to take care of some of that work," Lozar said.

Dusty didn't have to wonder what he meant.

VII

"Better play a card," Hunch whispered, slapping a card on the table himself.

Dusty nodded, glancing at Sitzman. He dropped a four of hearts on Hunch's ace of spades. Sitzman grinned and dropped a club on the top of the heap, shoving it all toward Hunch.

Dusty shot a glance at Usta and Lozar. If they could see these cards being played, they'd know how little the players were thinking of their game. He'd try to follow the lead suit after this, at least. But his ears and mind were tuned to the table farther over.

"First, we've got to make sure that money gets here," one of the men at that table said.

Usta nodded. "Right. After what just happened, those farmers may get ideas about holding up that buckboard we've got coming."

"Maybe we should ride out and escort it in," Lozar suggested.

"Exactly what we'll do," Usta agreed. "They may not know about it coming but we can't afford to take the chance."

"I hope they don't know," Lozar said, frowning. "I don't mind an open fight. But I don't care about being ambushed."

"Look who's talking," the other man said.

Lozar's hand dropped to his hip and the other man held up an open hand. "Don't be so touchy."

"Let's get out of here," Usta said. "We'll round up some of the boys and meet that buckboard far enough out that the farmers won't have a chance of getting to it first."

The men got up and Dusty looked at his own table, seeing it was his turn to play so he slapped a card down as the men filed out. He stole a glance at the men to see if they suspected that their words had been overheard. They seemed to be so engrossed with their immediate task that they didn't even glance at the three men playing cards.

"What are you going to do about that?" Sitzman asked as Usta's men went out the door and turned south toward Nettles Grocery Store.

Dusty shrugged. "Nothing. It's their money. Besides, protection of that money is not my responsibility until it gets into town."

Dusty thought he saw disappointment in Sitzman but the gambler had such a good poker face that he couldn't be sure. Dusty wondered about Sitzman. He appeared very eager to help and Dusty wasn't about to refuse any help when he could get it. There were too many unanswered questions as it was.

He thought of the watch he was looking for but decided against mentioning that. He had to know exactly where a man stood and know that he would never give away his confidence before he dared say anything about the watch. He certainly didn't know that much about Sitzman yet. And somehow he doubted if he ever would.

Dusty and Hunch abandoned the sham of the game they had been playing and got up from the table. Dusty was about to leave the saloon when he saw Tom Nettles come in and head straight for the bar. He was a little surprised. He hadn't pegged Nettles as a drinking man.

"He's scared spitless," Hunch whispered to Dusty.

Dusty nodded. "Usta probably reminded him that his money was going to be stored in the safe at his grocery. That could get him in plenty of trouble with the farmers. I figure Nettles is the kind who likes to stay out of trouble."

"Then he shouldn't bunch up with the likes of Usta and his gunmen," Hunch said softly. "Their middle name is trouble."

Dusty rubbed his stomach. "Do you suppose Molly would have any breakfast left? We missed that this morning, you know. And it's almost nine o'clock."

"Let's find out," Hunch said.

As they went out the door, Dusty glanced back. The saloon was practically empty now but it had been bustling with activity. "I'll bet Gumpy hasn't had that much business this early in the morning for a long time."

"I reckon everybody knew that stage was bringing in the money for the dam and they expected something big to happen. Even the bank opened an hour early to be ready for that money."

They crossed the street and went past the bank on their way to the boarding house. Dusty figured they'd get a tongue lashing from Molly for missing breakfast. Then they'd get something to eat, if he was any judge of Molly's generosity.

At the boarding house, they found Queeny Renick talking to Molly. Dusty looked around for Jennie but neither the teacher nor her dog was in sight. They'd gone to school, he decided.

"I wish there was a hotel in town," Queeny said as Dusty and Hunch stepped up on the porch. "This place smells like a skunk."

"Don't complain to me," Molly said indignantly. "Talk to the skunks about that. Jennie's dog tangled with a passel of them last night. Jennie scrubbed him but I reckon she picked up a little of the smell doing it. If you can't stand the smell, maybe you'd better go down to the saloon and see if they'll let you sleep in the back room."

"I'll get used to it, I suppose," Queeny said resignedly. "What choice do I have of rooms."

"None," Molly said. "There's just one room left."

Dusty and Hunch stepped into the big room then. Queeny wheeled on them, her face widening in a smile.

"So you're staying here, too? That makes the place seem much nicer."

"Hmp!" Molly snorted. "Don't know what's so nice about them. Had to get them an extra supper last night near midnight. Now they probably want me to get them some breakfast."

"We wouldn't mind having something to eat," Dusty said.

"You knew when breakfast was served," Molly snapped.

"We were quite a way from here at that time helping Craig Usta and Zeke Torberg prevent a stage hold-up."

Molly's face broke into a grin. "I heard about that. I don't know how you worked it but I would have given a side of beef to have seen their faces."

"Does that rate anything to eat?" Dusty asked.

"I reckon it does," Molly said. "Come on into the kitchen. I'll give you some breakfast but blamed if I'm going to set the table for you at nine o'clock. Have you had breakfast, Queeny?"

"No, I haven't," she said. "The stage driver said we could eat at the restaurant at the north end of town but I got off at the store."

"Well, you might as well eat, too," Molly said.

Molly set enough food on the kitchen table to feed an army, it seemed to Dusty. He liked the cold ham but cold fried eggs was not his favorite dish.

"Figured I'd give those eggs to Napoleon if you didn't show up for a late breakfast," Molly said. "Anything you don't eat, that dog gets."

She went into the other room to do her work, leaving Dusty and Hunch and Queeny to their late breakfast. Queeny dug into the bread and ham but turned up her nose at the cold eggs.

"I'll bet you've seen times when those cold eggs would have looked good to you," Dusty said.

Queeny frowned at him. "What makes you think you know so much about me?"

"We all see times like that," Dusty said easily. "Think you'll get the job at the saloon?"

"I've already got it," Queeny said. "Gumpy may not know it, but he'll find out when I get there tonight to sing."

"You may not get paid," Hunch said.

"I'll get paid, too," Queeny said.

Dusty didn't doubt it. Queeny Renick struck him as a woman who usually got what she wanted. And when she didn't, those who stood in her way would be sorry they did.

"I'm glad the marshal is boarding here," Queeny said. "I'll feel safer. But I'd like to know just what is going on. I know you and the deputy don't see eye to eye. And that bunch was trying to hold up the stage and kill everybody on it this morning till something happened. What was that?"

"We happened," Dusty said. "They had ideas about robbing the stage but they didn't want witnesses."

"How long has that banker been here in Jawbone?" Queeny asked.

Dusty shrugged. "I have no idea. Longer than we have, that's sure. We just pulled in yesterday."

Dusty wondered why Queeny had singled out Phoebus Pettigrew. Maybe he had looked out of place getting that money off the stage this morning and had attracted her attention.

"We'd better get back to town," Dusty said as soon as he and Hunch had finished their meal. "The marshal should be on the job."

"I'll see you tonight at the saloon if not before," Queeny said sweetly as they left.

"I can't imagine why Queeny decided to go into business in a town like Jawbone," Dusty said thoughtfully as he and Hunch went back toward the bank.

They were about to turn across the street to the deputy's office where Dusty figured on headquartering when Fred Yoeman stopped them. The hardware man was coming down the street from his store.

"We've having a meeting immediately in the back room of the bank," Yoeman said. "We want you there."

"What's wrong now?"

"You'll find out at the meeting," Yoeman said and went on into the bank.

Dusty hesitated a minute then followed the hardware man inside. He was surprised when he stepped into the back room to find the two farmers he had met yesterday, Ed Klosson and Orlo Quill, already there. Phoebus Pettigrew was there but he was pacing back and forth nervously instead of sitting in his big chair at the desk. Dusty glanced around. Serg Sitzman, the gambler, wasn't here, so this must not be a town council meeting.

Pettigrew moved over and closed the door to the lobby of the bank. "Now then," he said, "let's get down to business. Had you heard that the ranchers are bringing in some money to pay their hired guns?"

Dusty nodded. "I heard about it. But it doesn't make sense. Surely they can afford to hire a few gunmen without having to borrow the money."

Pettigrew went to his chair at the desk. "The way I get it, the ranchers have formed a sort of association to get rid of the farmers along the river. I figure Craig Usta is the association. This new organization is hiring the gunmen. I don't know whether the association is borrowing the money to pay them or whether Craig Usta has his money banked somewhere else and has to send for it. He sure doesn't keep any in my bank."

Dusty nodded. Usta probably didn't trust Nettles' safe, either. So, unless he was willing to keep cash at his ranch, he probably did have his money banked in some other town.

"What does this have to do with us?"

"Plenty," Orlo Quill said. "I figure if we can get that money, the ranchers won't be so high handed. If they can't pay their hired guns, they'll quit. Once they're gone, we can handle the ranchers and their regular hands. At least, we can with the help of Wolfe's construction crew."

Dusty frowned. "Are you suggesting we rob the buckboard bringing in their money?"

"So you've heard it is coming in a buckboard?" Klosson said. "I see you find out things. What's wrong with that idea? They tried to steal our money, didn't they?"

"The first thing that is wrong with it is that you'll probably wind up in a pitched battle with those gunmen you're so afraid of," Dusty said.

"We'll hold up the buckboard before it gets to town," Quill said.

"They're going to meet that buckboard and escort it in," Dusty retorted.

Yoeman shook his head. "That's not so good. But I still think we have to get that money. Without pay, those gunmen will quit in a minute. If Usta does send an escort to meet that buckboard, he probably won't send many. We'll take every available man and surprise them. I still vote for it."

Dusty looked at Pettigrew. The banker was worried but he nodded. "We have to strike quickly or they may kill us all. This looks like the best bet and probably the safest one."

"I vote against it," Dusty said, remembering Usta's determination when he'd seen him last in the saloon.

"You're out-voted," Pettigrew said. "We're depending on you to help us. That's what you were hired to do."

Dusty thought of several arguments he could use but decided against all of them. These men were as determined as Usta was. All Dusty and Hunch wanted was to find Matt Dekin's killer and Hunch's money. Opposing these men wasn't going to help their cause any.

"We'll have to leave here by noon," Quill said. "We'll get Wolfe's men to go with us. They're as interested in this as we are."

Quill and Klosson went out, followed by Fred Yoeman. Dusty and Hunch started after them.

"You'll ride with us," Pettigrew said. "Don't forget!"

VIII

Phoebus Pettigrew watched Dusty Dekin and his sidekick, Hunch Huckle, leave his office. He was still far from convinced that Dusty could or would do the job he had expected of the son of Matt Dekin. Some of the others, Ed Klosson in particular, seemed to think that Dusty was just the man they wanted.

Of course, what they wanted Dusty to do and what Pettigrew wanted were two different things, although they didn't know it. The farmers simply wanted Dusty to make sure nothing stopped the building of the dam. Judging from what Pettigrew had seen of the way Dusty operated, he just might succeed in that.

But Pettigrew wanted a few men eliminated, particularly Craig Usta. Usta had been the big man along Dreary River when Pettigrew came to Jawbone. He still was and he would be until something happened to him. Pettigrew's ambitions would be cramped as long as Usta was the kingpin.

Now that Usta had brought in gunmen like Ben Lozar, Dusty would probably have to get rid of the gunmen before he could even get to Usta. It was a big job, too big for a man who didn't even carry a gun. Dusty Dekin was a real disappointment to Pettigrew.

Pettigrew got up to go into the main lobby of the bank to talk to his teller. But the partition door opened and Ed Klosson came back in.

"I forgot one thing I came in for this morning,"

Klosson said. "Guess I was too busy thinking about that money Usta is bringing in. I got the rest of the signatures on this paper for the loan from the bank."

He dug a paper out of his shirt pocket and handed it to Pettigrew. Pettigrew nodded in satisfaction.

"Fine, Ed. Now the bank can loan you the rest of the money you'll need to build your dam. I have all the money on hand now since I got that shipment this morning."

"We'll pay it back once we get that dam in," Klosson promised.

Klosson went back outside and Pettigrew stuck his head through the partition door. No customers were in the bank at the moment.

"I'll be back in a few minutes," he said to his teller then ducked back into his office. Crossing to the door that opened into the alley, he went outside and moved up the alley to the rear of the hardware store.

Pettigrew tried the rear door of the hardware. Sometimes Fred kept this locked but today it wasn't. He opened the door and stepped into the dim interior. He didn't like this room. Fred Yoeman always kept a coffin or two here since the town had no undertaker and Fred made all the coffins that were needed.

Pettigrew hurried through the back room into the main part of the store. There were no customers and he was glad of that. He had some things to talk over with Fred in private.

"I got the signatures that Ed Klosson promised me," he announced to the hardware man. "Now we can put that with the mortgages we have and we've got every-thing along the creek tied up."

Yoeman grinned. "Sounds good. I never heard of taking mortgages on land a man has filed on but hasn't even moved onto yet."

"I checked with a lawyer," Pettigrew said. "He told me this paper I made out would be legal if those fel-lows who have filed on the land along the river would sign it. And they did. Ed just brought it to me. It came in on the stage this morning. So now we'll let them have the money they need to build their dam."

Yoeman nodded. "And close them out before they can make a dime off their dam."

"Exactly," Pettigrew said. He and Fred Yoeman had the same ambitions and neither had any compunctions about how they went about accomplishing their ends. Pettigrew had thought he had enough money to handle the banking affairs of Jawbone. But when Klosson and Quill came to him with this expensive dam project, he hadn't been able to handle that alone. Fred Yoeman had been eager to step in as Pettigrew's partner to finance it. Both could see the great advantages of owning the lowlands along Dreary River both up and downstream from Jawbone.

"If we handle this just right, we could wind up with the ranches north of town, too," Yoeman said. "Once the dam is in, these farmers will take over all the meadow land and the ranchers will have their tails in a crack because they won't have any winter feed."

"We're going to have to pinch off the farmers at

exactly the right time then we can put the squeeze on the ranchers," Pettigrew agreed.

"For now, we've got to keep the ranchers from stopping this dam project," Yoeman said. "If they stop that, they'll keep control of this valley and our whole plan will be dead. We'll even lose the money we've put into these loans."

Pettigrew nodded. "You're right. If we can stop that money Usta is bringing in, that should put a crimp in the ranchers' plans. When the dam is almost finished, we might even let the farmers and ranchers have their little war. If there are enough farmers to handle the ranchers, it will make it easier for us to take over the ranches once we foreclose on the farms."

"We think alike, Phoebus," Yoeman said. "It would help if we could get our marshal to eliminate Ben Lozar and maybe another one or two of Usta's gun slingers."

"What's he going to kill them with, a slingshot?" Pettigrew grumbled.

Pettigrew went out the front door and almost bumped into his wife on her way to Nettles Grocery Store.

"I'm glad I met you here," she said quickly. "I was just going to stop at the bank. I've got to have more money if we are to have anything decent to eat."

Pettigrew scowled. "We're hard run at the bank after loaning all that money to the farmers," he grumbled. "You know that. Why can't you get along like you did when we were first married?"

"Things are higher priced now," she snapped. "But it's all right with me if you want to eat corn meal mush three times a day."

"Aw, shut up," Pettigrew snapped as a passing woman turned to look at them. He didn't want their family squabbles exposed to the gossips of town. He took a five dollar bill from his pocket. "Here. Buy what you need. I'll expect a good dinner when I come home today."

"I'm out of almost everything at the house," she said. "If this isn't enough, I'll come by the bank for more."

He sucked in his breath to tell her to make that do or he'd just eat at the restaurant. But he checked himself. She was already moving away and the only way he could make her hear would be to shout. He wasn't going to do that.

Wheeling, he went down the street and into the bank. His teller was just finishing with a customer and he came out from behind his window.

"Mr. Pettigrew, I promised my wife I'd bring her some things from the store if I could be spared for a few minutes," he said. "She isn't feeling well today."

Pettigrew nodded. "Go ahead," he said.

He often wondered if he couldn't save some money if he did all the bank work himself. There really wasn't a great deal to do in a town the size of Jawbone. But he didn't like to be tied down every minute the bank was open. And he didn't like all the book work after hours. His teller did that. When he considered his freedom to go where he pleased at any time, he decided the teller was worth the wages he earned.

He saw the teller go across the street to the grocery. Then he turned his attention to the front door as he heard it open. His jaw dropped as he saw Queeny Renick come in and close the door.

"What are you doing here?" he gasped.

"This is a public business, isn't it?" Queeny said in that syrup smooth voice he remembered so well.

"Sure, but you don't have any business here."

"That's where you're as wrong as you have ever been, Phoebus," she said.

Pettigrew inched his way back to the gate leading behind the counter. He guessed he'd known she'd show up here ever since he had seen her get off the stage this morning. But he'd tried to tell himself that it wouldn't happen.

"You can't have any business with me," he repeated. "I just run a bank."

Queeny moved up to the window and smiled through the bars. "You don't 'just' do anything, Phoeby, unless there is a lot of money in it for you. Remember I got pretty well acquainted with you in Denver when you were only a teller in a bank. About three nights a week. You even told me how you were accumulating all that money but you slipped out without telling me where you were going."

"I paid for those nights," Pettigrew said uneasily. "What more do you want?"

"I think you could use a partner in your scheme here."

"I don't have any scheme," Pettigrew denied, wondering if she had any idea what he and Fred Yoeman were doing.

Queeny leaned on the counter. "Look, Phoeby," she said softly. "I've a room at Molly Guzek's boarding house. You know how Molly likes to talk and how much she knows. I know what she knows now."

Pettigrew's heart turned to a lump of lead. Nobody but Fred Yoeman knew about his scheme, he had told himself over and over. But if anybody had figured out something was afoot, it would be Molly. And for a clever woman like Queeny, it would be a simple task to get that information from Molly if she knew it.

"You're helping the farmers build a dam so they can settle this land," Queeny said easily. "Knowing you, that means you're going to grab that land with the mortgages you're taking. Likely you'll have the ranchers broke by that time so you can grab the ranches, too. That's good, Phoeby. I'll help you do it. But I want my share."

Pettigrew knew his face was revealing how accurate Queeny's guess was. He had learned from experience that he couldn't hide much from her. But he also knew that she would take everything before she was finished if he let her get a finger in the pie. He had to get rid of her some way.

"How could you help?" Pettigrew asked, his voice hoarse in spite of his determination to control it.

"Well, you need a happy frame of mind to keep alert for this job. I doubt if your nights at home are any better than they used to be. Now—"

Pettigrew held up his hand. "Nothing doing. I'm not starting that again. I almost didn't save enough money to start this bank because of you. I'm not—"

He broke off as he saw his wife coming across the street from the grocery store. She was after more money. But that was a minor problem for him now. Queeny was a big one.

"Here comes my wife," he said, the words choking in his throat. "You've got to get out of here."

"She knew about me in Denver, I understand."

"That's why I left there." He looked around frantically. If she could go through his office and out the rear door—but there wasn't time. His eyes fell on the big vault where the door was partly open.

"Into the vault," he snapped and grabbed her arm, pulling her around the counter and through the little gate.

Before she could object, he shoved her through the vault door and shoved the big door closed. He hadn't gotten the handle turned when his wife came in.

"What are you doing in the vault, Phoebus?" she asked as if she had caught a child in the cookie jar.

"Just putting something valuable in there for safe keeping," Pettigrew said, hoping his voice wasn't quivering like he was.

He listened for Queeny to begin shouting and pounding. The vault was solid but he doubted if it was sound proof. But everything was quiet. Then a new fear hit him. Suppose Queeny couldn't breathe in there. He almost wished she was dead. But he didn't want her to die in his bank vault.

"You'll have to open that vault again," Mrs. Pettigrew said. "I need more money."

"How much?"

"At least ten dollars," she said.

Pettigrew reached into the cash drawer under the counter and got a ten dollar bill and handed it to his wife. He saw the surprise in her face.

"Something's wrong," she said suspiciously. "You never gave me this much before without a fight."

"I've got a lot of work to do and no time for arguing," he said. He came out from behind the counter and took her arm. "Why don't you go back to the store and buy what you need?"

Shaking her head, Mrs. Pettigrew went outside and across the street, looking back twice before she reached the porch of the store. Pettigrew waited impatiently until she disappeared in the store then he ran to the vault and worked the combination, swinging the door open. The breath whistled out of his lungs when he saw Queeny standing there grinning at him.

"It's dark in here, you know," she said. "We'll find a place that isn't quite this dark when you call for me tonight."

"I'm not calling for you tonight," Pettigrew said, his relief at finding her all right and not mad enough to kill him mingled with his renewed fear of what was to come.

"You pick the night," Queeny said. She made her way leisurely to the door and out into the street.

Pettigrew watched her, doubts gnawing him. She couldn't have changed that much. The way he remembered her in Denver, she should have come out of that vault clawing and biting like a wildcat with his tail in a trap.

Suddenly a thought hit him. He dashed to the vault, which he hadn't closed again, and went inside. Pushing the door wide open to let in the light, he ran his hands over the shelves where the paper money was kept. There was one big gap in the row of bills. That's why Queeny was so good natured. She had stolen all the paper money she could hide under her dress.

Running out of the vault, he almost bumped into his teller coming back to work. Yelling at him to watch the bank, he dashed out into the street. His first glance caught Dusty Dekin and Hunch Huckle up in front of the hardware store. He ran that way.

The marshal saw him coming and stopped, obviously startled to see the town banker running like this.

"What happened to you?" Dusty demanded. "Somebody rob your bank?"

Pettigrew nodded. "Exactly. While my back was turned, this new woman, Queeny Renick, got into my vault. She took a lot of the money that came in this morning. That's the money to pay for the dam."

Dusty whistled. "I didn't figure she was clever enough to rob your bank while you were right there. I suppose you want me to get it back?"

"I sure do," Pettigrew said. "If you don't get it, the farmers won't be able to build their dam."

IX

Dusty stared at Phoebus Pettigrew as he wheeled and almost ran back to his bank. It was almost funny to think that Pettigrew had let Queeny rob him while he was right there.

"I reckon our wages depends on getting that money back for Pettigrew," Dusty said.

Hunch nodded. "If that woman got into the vault, I'll bet she took plenty. Could be she did take enough to stop the contractors from working."

Dusty sighed. "I didn't figure on having to run down female bank robbers but it's the unexpected things that makes this job so attractive. Let's go see if she hid it in her room at the boarding house."

"She hasn't had time to do that, has she?" Hunch asked. "Of course, Pettigrew didn't say how long ago she robbed him."

"Maybe he doesn't know just when she did get it," Dusty said. "If it isn't in her room at Molly's place, she probably still has it on her."

When they got to the boarding house, they found Molly in the kitchen getting dinner.

"Don't tell me you're not going to be here for dinner," Molly shouted belligerently. "I'll feed you poison if you come in late again."

Dusty held up his hand. "We solemnly promise to be here for dinner. What we want to know now is whether Queeny has been back since she left after breakfast."

97

Molly snorted. "Pretty late breakfast! And she hasn't been back."

"She couldn't have slipped in without you seeing her?" Molly shook her head and Dusty led Hunch back outside.

"She must still have the money with her. It's not likely she'll hide it anywhere around town. So now that we have a good idea where it is, we have to make sure she doesn't get a chance to hide it."

"But if she's got it on her, how do you figure on getting it? Strip her?"

Dusty shook his head, an idea coming to him. "I'll let her strip herself."

"Whoa!" Hunch snorted. "Count me out of this. I didn't think you were the kind, Dusty."

"You're jumping at conclusions, Hunch," Dusty said reproachfully, his mind whirling with his idea. "Look. Here she comes."

"I hope you don't figure on making her strip right here," Hunch grunted.

"Go down to the livery barn and get my horse and rent another one with a side-saddle," Dusty ordered.

Hunch nodded and angled toward the livery barn, looking back once and shaking his head. Dusty moved out to the walk leading down toward the bank and stopped, waiting for Queeny.

"Wondered if you'd like to ride out and see a little of the country," Dusty invited when Queeny reached him.

She looked at him suspiciously. "Didn't think you

were interested in showing me anything but the way out of town," she said.

"Everybody gets terrible ideas about me," Dusty complained.

"Too bad that you are misjudged so," she said. "I like to see what is around a town where I work. Buggy or horseback?"

"I've sent Hunch for a couple of horses, one with a side-saddle."

Queeny pursed her lips. "You are confident. What if I won't go?"

"I'll take Hunch for a ride. He can ride side-saddle."

Queeny laughed. "I like your answers. I think it might be interesting to ask you some more questions."

Hunch came from the livery barn, leading two horses. He shook his head once at Dusty as he handed the reins to him but he didn't say anything.

Dusty helped Queeny mount then he swung up. "How about down by the river?" he asked.

She nodded. "Race you?" she shouted and kicked her horse into a run.

They headed south behind the feed store, crossing a corner of the school playground. He shot a glance at the school house and was sure he saw a face at the window. That would be Jennie. She wouldn't think much of his taking Queeny for a ride. But then she didn't think much of anything he did.

Dusty caught up with Queeny before they reached the river and they slowed their horses to a walk. His mind was working rapidly, wondering how he was going to implement the idea he had.

There were a few native plum bushes along the banks of the river and a couple of hackberry trees. At one place, a little above the spot where they were going to reach the river, someone had planted a small grove of cottonwood trees. These trees, close to the water, had shot up until they were already good sized.

The horses seemed eager to get to the water and Dusty guessed they hadn't been watered this morning. It gave him an idea how to manage things.

"Looks like the horses want a drink," he said. "Let's get down and let them have some water."

Queeny shrugged. "All right."

At the water's edge, Dusty swung down then helped Queeny dismount. Just as she was about to touch the ground, he jabbed a thumb into the flank of Queeny's horse. The horse snorted and shied to one side, jerking Queeny off balance. They were right at the water's edge. Dusty made a gallant effort to catch Queeny but succeeded only in shoving her farther toward the water. She stumbled and splashed headlong into the water.

Dusty let the horse go and reached out to grab Queeny's hand and pull her to dry land. The water was shallow here but the mud was deep. Her clothes were soaked and plastered with mud.

"I can't ride back into town looking like this," she wailed.

"Sure wouldn't help the reputation of the new singer at the saloon to be seen like that," Dusty agreed.

"You clumsy ox!" she yelled, turning her wrath on Dusty. "You should have kept that horse from jumping."

Dusty nodded meekly. "I reckon I should have. But nobody told me he was going to do that. I'll ride back to the boarding house and get a clean dress for you. How about that?"

Queeny nodded, evidently placated by Dusty's concern. He was thankful she hadn't seen him nudge that horse.

"I'm muddy all the way through," she moaned. "I need to take a bath."

Dusty pointed to the cottonwoods. "There's a good pool of water right by those cottonwoods. You could strip off in those trees and take a dip while I get your clean dress."

"Good idea," Queeny said. She headed for the cottonwoods while Dusty led the horses to the trees where he tied Queeny's horse. "No fair peeking," she shouted at him while he tied the horse.

Instead of mounting and heading for the boarding house, Dusty waited until he heard Queeny splashing in the water. Then he hurried into the grove until he found her clothes. There was nothing but mud on her dress but he found a big roll of bills in a pocket in her petticoat. He was just taking the money when Queeny discovered him.

"You black hearted thief!" she screamed. "I'll kill you!"

Dusty grinned at Queeny with just her head sticking

101

out of the water. "I'm only taking what you took from the bank. If I got more than what you took, you can get it back from Pettigrew."

"I'll claw your eyes out!" she screamed at him.

"Just enjoy your bath," Dusty said. "I'll bring you a clean dress."

"I'll kill you when I get out of here!" she yelled.

Dusty rolled the muddy dress up into a ball and took it with him. He didn't want Queeny coming after him until he delivered the money and she wasn't liable to chase him in her petticoat. He rode directly to the boarding house and asked Molly to get a clean dress out of Queeny's room. He handed her the muddy one.

"You must have left her in pretty shape," Molly sputtered, taking the dress and going up the stairs. She was back in a minute and handed him a clean dress.

As Dusty was leaving the house, he met Jennie coming from school for something she must have forgotten this morning. She saw the dress and her eyes widened in amazement. He tried to ignore her, knowing he could never explain this to Jennie.

Riding back to the cottonwoods, he spread the dress over a low tree limb. The rest of Queeny's clothes were wet but most of the mud had been on the dress.

"Hope you had a nice swim," Dusty said.

"I'll get even with you!" Queeny promised.

"I've got to see my banker right now," Dusty said and wheeled his horse back toward town.

At the bank, he reined up and went inside, putting the money on Pettigrew's desk in his office.

Pettigrew stared at him in disbelief. "I didn't think you'd get it," he said. "And certainly not this quick."

"It had to be quick before she had time to hide it," Dusty said. "I took all she was carrying in that pocket in her petticoat. If you've got more here than she took from the bank, it would be gentlemanly of you to give her own money back to her."

Pettigrew gasped. "From her petticoat?" He shook his head, a trace of a grin on his face. "You're an amazing man, Dusty."

"I'm liable to be a dead one the next time she sees me," Dusty said.

"In half an hour, Quill and Klosson are leading the men out to intercept Usta's money wagon," Pettigrew said, bringing Dusty back to the problem he'd had before Queeny robbed the bank. "You're to go with them."

Dusty nodded and went outside to his horse. He rode up to the boarding house just in time for the noon meal.

"Figured you'd be here this time," Molly said. "Looked to me like you had a busy morning and would need some dinner."

Dusty and Hunch ate fast. Queeny wasn't at the table. Maybe she had waited at the river to dry off. Dusty wanted to be gone before she showed up. He had another reason for hurrying, too. He had to get down to the bank and see if he could stop this attempt at holding up that buckboard. He knew there would be plenty of Usta's men with that wagon and the result was sure to be a pitched battle.

Through the window, Dusty saw Queeny riding slowly up from the river and he and Hunch finished their meal and hurried out the door.

"I'll take Queeny's horse back to the stable after she gets here and saddle my own horse," Hunch said. "You'd better be gone before she arrives."

Dusty nodded and rode down to the bank. Orlo Quill and Ed Klosson were already there. Fred Yoeman was there, too, but it was obvious he wasn't going to ride with them. Yoeman's two hundred and twenty pounds would be a big load for a horse to carry, anyway. There were several other men there and Vyrl Wolfe came out of the bank just as Dusty rode up.

"You're heading into a big fight," Dusty warned. "I overheard Usta tell Ben Lozar to take several men and meet this buckboard. We don't want a war."

"Maybe we do," Quill said. "We've got to fight them sometime. Might as well be when there's something worth fighting for. That money should be."

Wolfe spoke up. "We've got to stop that money from reaching the ranchers, Dusty. If those gunmen don't get their pay, they'll ride on. Then we can build our dam in peace. We won't get much done while they're around."

Dusty saw the logic in that. But he knew the odds would be against the farmers even with most of Wolfe's construction crew riding with them. They weren't gunmen. Most of Usta's men were.

Dusty started to object again but Quill motioned

toward the road and spurred his horse. The others followed. Dusty's horse jumped forward, too, but he checked him. Hunch was just coming up from the livery barn with his horse.

"You'll lose half your men out there today," he warned Wolfe.

"We can't have that," Pettigrew said worriedly. "Can't you help them, Dusty?"

Dusty rubbed his chin. "I'm working on an idea. I don't like to see that money reach Usta. But I'd hate worse to see half of the construction crew killed."

Hunch reached him then and Dusty motioned for him to follow. He rode up the side street toward the boarding house.

"You'll have a war of your own if you run into that woman," Hunch warned.

"Can't be helped. Molly has something I think we can use to break up that fight between the ranchers and farmers."

Hunch shrugged. He had learned to wait until Dusty's plans developed before asking too many questions.

Dusty went into the house cautiously but Queeny was not in sight.

"She went up to get into some dry things," Molly explained. "She said she was soaked to the skin and you didn't take her any skin garments. What brought you back here?"

"I thought I saw an old bear hide out in the shed behind the house," Dusty said. "Wondered if I could borrow it."

"I wish you'd take the stinking thing out and bury it," Molly said. "Jim killed that bear years ago but he didn't get the hide cured right. It still stinks."

"How about some bear grease?" Dusty asked. "I know you've got some of that."

"Sure have," Molly said. "It stinks, too, but it's good for a cold. What do you want with a bear skin and bear grease? Going hunting?"

Dusty nodded. "Sort of. Big game, too."

X

"I reckon I'm pretty stupid," Hunch said as he helped Dusty tie the bear skin on behind the saddle of his horse. "I don't quite see what you need a bear skin for."

"My horse doesn't see the need, either," Dusty said, trying to calm his horse which had caught the scent of the skin.

"Maybe he's smarter than you are," Hunch said.

"Help me get on this spooked critter," Dusty said. "I'll explain it all to you as we ride. We've got a lot to do before those ranchers meet up with Quill's ambush."

Hunch shook his head. "A bear skin and bear grease. If you were heading for Alaska to spend the winter, that might make sense."

Dusty got his horse under control but the horse didn't like his burden and he let his rider know it. Dusty guided him down to the livery stable and reined up.

"Watch this horse for me, will you, Hunch? He's plenty spooky."

"Can't say I blame him," Hunch said. But he grabbed the reins and held the horse's head close to the flank of his own horse.

Dusty went inside and found the stable owner. "You said the other day that you never got a chance to rent out that burro. You've got a chance now. How much do you want for him for about two or three hours?"

The livery stable man looked at Dusty in disbelief. "You can have Old Golddust for the rest of time for a dollar."

Dusty took out a dollar and handed it to the man. "It's only for this afternoon," he said.

The livery man got a rope and caught the burro and brought him to Dusty. "He don't move very fast."

"He'll have to speed up a little. But we're not going to ride him."

Taking him outside, he handed the long rope to Hunch. "Hang on to him tight. You'll have to lead him. He doesn't like the smell of bears, you know."

Hunch nodded. "So you're going to use this burro and that bear skin to ruin somebody's party." He scratched an ear with the end of the rope. "When you mix them together, that's liable to cause quite a commotion."

"I hope so," Dusty said. "Let's go."

Dusty had trouble mounting again. His horse still disagreed with Dusty's decision to take along the bear skin and had not given up the argument.

"You'd better take the lead, Hunch," Dusty said. "We're heading into the wind. Don't want Golddust to get a whiff of this bear skin until we're ready."

"I'm not sure I'll ever be ready for that," Hunch said but he nudged his horse into a trot on the road leading west along the north bank of the river. Dusty followed.

"Where are we going?" Hunch called back after they had passed Ed Klosson's homestead.

"Same place we were this morning," Dusty said. "Orlo Quill plans to wait in those rocks for the buckboard."

Dusty wondered how far ahead Quill and his men were. They had left town before he got the bear skin. And how far away was the buckboard? If it got to those rocks at the river crossing before Dusty was ready, it would mean a pitched battle between the two forces and a lot of men would likely be killed. Control of this valley wasn't worth that.

He called to Hunch to hurry but Hunch was having trouble getting any speed out of the burro. When the rocks came in sight, Dusty motioned for Hunch to turn down a gully and come into the rocks beyond the ambush point. The burro was getting tired and pulled back on his lead rope harder all the time.

When Hunch finally rode into the rocks and stopped, Dusty reined in well behind him.

"This donkey is too tired to perform for you now," Hunch said.

"One whiff of this bear skin will revive him."

Dusty found a sharp rock outcropping and tied his

108

horse to it. Climbing quickly to a spot where he could scan the road to the south of the river crossing, he settled down to wait for the appearance of the buckboard. Looking back, he searched the rocks beyond Hat Rock and caught a glimpse or two of movement. Klosson's men were just about where he had expected them to be. Dusty's timing would have to be almost perfect if his plan was to succeed.

He searched the rocks until he located the horses of Klosson's men in a pocket just beneath their ambush where they could get to them quickly if they needed them for a chase.

Suddenly Dusty tensed and squinted his eyes against the sun's glare as he stared to the south. A cloud of dust was rising there. It was a lot of dust for one wagon. The escort that had ridden out to meet the buckboard must have made contact and was coming back now with it.

Dusty slid down from his looking post. "They're coming, Hunch. We've got to get ready."

"Doing what?" Hunch asked. "Introducing Golddust to that bear skin?"

Dusty nodded. "First, we're going to rub that skin well with bear grease."

"It already stinks to high heaven," Hunch said.

"The grease will make it stronger. Then we'll lash that skin on to the donkey and turn him loose out in the road."

Hunch grinned. "If that long-eared varmit is half as scared of bear smell as the livery man said he was, we'll see some show."

"So will Usta's men, I hope."

Dusty's horse snorted and shied away as Dusty untied the bear skin and pulled it from behind the saddle. Spreading out the skin, he uncapped the jar of bear grease and rubbed it on the skin. He couldn't blame the burro much for not liking that smell. It was sickening to Dusty.

"Watch these critters," Dusty warned and climbed back to his lookout perch. The buckboard was just on the south side of the river now and Dusty's eyes widened as he saw the size of the escort. He counted eleven riders. With the wagon driver, that made twelve men. Quill and Klosson didn't have more than eight. But Dusty was sure that Quill would try to take that money, anyway. He was too stubborn to let common sense change his mind.

As the first riders hit the ford, Dusty slid down from the rock and ran to the bear skin.

"It's time now," he said. "You grab that rope on the donkey and hang on. I'll put this skin on him."

Hunch shook his head but he grabbed the rope. "This ain't going to be easy."

Dusty picked up the bear skin. With it and a long rope, he approached Golddust. The donkey threw his long ears forward and watched Dusty suspiciously but he stood patiently until Dusty got close enough that he got a whiff of the bear skin. Then he wheeled and almost jerked Hunch off his feet in his effort to get away.

Dusty dashed in and slapped the skin on the donkey

110

then whipped the rope under his belly, dodging the flying hoofs to get a knot in the rope and pull it tight.

"This way," Dusty said and grabbed the rope with Hunch and began pulling the burro toward the road.

When they broke out of the rocks, the wagon was across the river and so were the riders. Dusty dodged back to Golddust and jabbed a rock under the bear skin directly beneath the rope so that it dug into the burro's back every time he moved. That added to the donkey's frenzy.

"Let him go!" Dusty said and gave the donkey a hard slap.

The burro leaped toward the road then stopped and began bucking. The bear skin flapped up and down, adding to the donkey's panic. With a terrified bray that could have been heard for miles, he bucked toward the road.

Dusty and Hunch dodged back into the rocks. Everything depended on Golddust now. The donkey showed no signs of disappointing them.

Apparently thinking that company might save him, Golddust headed for the riders leading the wagon, bucking and braying with every jump. Usta's men suddenly had more than they could handle directly under them. It might have been the bear smell that terrified the horses but Dusty guessed it was more likely the apparition created by the braying, bucking donkey coming directly at them, the bear skin flapping with every leap.

The horses exploded into bucking that rivaled the

antics of Golddust. The driver of the wagon got a firm grip on his reins but he couldn't hold his horses. They exploded into a dead run, dashing past the bucking horses and donkey because the wagon tongue wouldn't allow them to turn tail and run.

The horses behind the wagon joined the melee, all of them bucking up the road in the direction they had been going because the burro had gone through the riders and was now at their rear.

Golddust didn't want to be left alone in his time of trial, however, so he wheeled and followed the pitching horses. Dusty shot a glance at the rocks where Quill and Klosson and their men had been waiting. They had started down toward their own horses, apparently determined to run down the buckboard since their ambush was ruined.

But before they reached their horses, the animals either got wind of the bear smell or caught the excitement of the action and decided to join it. They jerked loose from the man holding them and began a bucking exhibition of their own, some going out into the road to join the other horses and some heading back for the familiar grounds of their own corrals.

"We'd better get out of here before we have them all shooting at us," Dusty suggested.

"That's the smartest thing you've said today," Hunch agreed. "They're pretty busy right now but that won't last forever."

Dusty and Hunch hurried back through the rocks. Their horses had caught the excitement but hadn't broken loose yet. Dusty and Hunch mounted and reined to the north, putting some distance between them and the scene of confusion behind. Finally Dusty swung back to the east.

"We'd better stay clear of that crowd till they get to town," Hunch cautioned.

"We've got to catch that donkey," Dusty explained. "Tired as he was, I figure he'll play out and stop running before he gets back to town. We've got to return him and that bear skin."

Dusty had guessed right. A mile from town they found Golddust, standing with head down, puffing as though there wasn't enough air in the world to fill his lungs. Dusty walked right up to him. Quickly he stripped the bear skin from his back and rolled it up. His problem then was to get on his own horse again. With Hunch's help, he made it.

Cautiously, they rode into town and stopped at the livery barn where Dusty returned the donkey. The livery man stared at the exhausted burro and shook his head but didn't say anything. Golddust would have plenty of time now to recuperate.

From the rear of the livery barn, Dusty looked up the alley to the back of Tom Nettles' store. The buckboard was there so the ranchers had gotten their money to town. That could mean more trouble but, at least, Dusty had prevented a battle out on the road today. Klosson and his men weren't back yet and wouldn't be for a while. It was quite a walk from the river ford into town.

Dusty and Hunch rode to the boarding house and Dusty put the bear skin back in the little shed behind the house. As they started past the house toward town, Molly came out on the porch.

"Did Old Bruin's hide do you any good?" she asked.

"It helped put on a big show," Dusty said.

"I'm not sure you'd better come to supper," Molly said.

Dusty rubbed his chin. "Why not?"

"First, because you smell like an over-ripe bear. And, second, Jennie is liable to shoot you."

"What for?" Dusty asked innocently.

"She thinks you and Queeny were into some mischief. Can't say that I blame her."

"You're both dead wrong," Dusty said. "Anyway, what I do is none of Jennie's business."

"That's exactly what she said. But when a girl says that something doesn't mean anything to her, it usually does mean something. You're skating on thin ice, Dusty, and she's got an ax."

Dusty grinned. "You tell her I'm ready and willing to help her with her school program tomorrow."

"She won't let you on the grounds!" Molly snorted.

Dusty and Hunch rode back to the livery barn and put their horses away. After washing up at the horse tank, they headed for the saloon. That was the only place where Dusty had seen the watch they were looking for. It seemed the most logical place to look for it again.

"Usta's men may be there," Hunch warned. "After the pounding that those bucking horses gave them, their bottoms will be sore. And a dog with a sore tail is sure to bite."

"We won't aggravate them," Dusty said. "I've been thinking about that watch. It disappeared mighty fast from that bar yesterday. Gumpy was serving a drink when I got back inside. Can you picture Gumpy Alvis as a killer?"

Hunch nodded thoughtfully. "Maybe. He's no angel, that's for sure."

"Let's check him out."

They went into the saloon. None of Usta's men were here now. They must be helping put the money into Nettles' safe, Dusty decided. Gumpy was behind the bar and Sitzman came over to them as soon as they appeared.

"Looks like you've had a hard ride," he said. "Have you seen the wagon down behind Tom Nettles' store?"

Dusty nodded. "We've seen it." He watched Sitzman closely. He was being overly friendly again. There had to be a reason but Dusty just couldn't put his finger on it.

XI

Serg Sitzman was a suspicious man by nature and he recognized suspicion in another man. He saw it in Dusty Dekin right now. He'd have to be very careful. Somehow he had to find out exactly what Dusty and his partner were doing in Jawbone. He couldn't believe Dusty had come just to be marshal of the town. No man who wouldn't wear a gun looked for jobs like that.

He watched Dusty move around the saloon, saying something to Queeny and nearly getting his head snapped off then talking a minute with Gumpy at the bar. Could it be that he was suspicious of Gumpy? That was something Sitzman would have to watch. Gumpy's tongue wasn't loose but the brain hooked to it was.

When Dusty and his partner finally left the saloon, Sitzman moved down to the far end of the bar and leaned there, motioning with his eyes for Gumpy to come over. Business was slow with only two customers besides Queeny.

"What were they talking about?" he asked Gumpy. "Did they get personal with their questions?"

Gumpy shook his head. "Didn't say much. But I didn't like the way they looked around at everything. Like they expected to see something."

"Maybe they did," Sitzman said. "We've got to make sure they don't find anything. We can't afford to let them get suspicious of us."

He turned around so that he could face the outside door as well as see everyone inside the saloon. The man at the far end of the bar set his empty glass down and went outside. That only left Queeny at a table along the distant wall fingering some cards and a lone drinker at a table close to her. The saloon was as near deserted as it ever was this time of day.

"Now that the money has come into Nettles', we

won't have to wait much longer, will we?" Gumpy asked softly.

Sitzman shook his head. "No. But we can't get in too big of a sweat, either. Everything must be planned out right."

He looked at the bartender. He had told everybody when they first came here that Gumpy was the owner of the saloon and he was just a gambler. But he guessed that some suspected that he was really the owner and Gumpy the hired hand. Maybe it wasn't too important. But he wanted to keep their real identities hidden.

Until the birth of this wild scheme of a dam across Dreary River and the influx of farmers, there had been little danger of outsiders coming here. Soon now they'd be swarming in. It was time for Gumpy and him to get out. But they wouldn't go empty-handed; not with all the money both the farmers and ranchers had brought in.

Gumpy carelessly wiped the bar. "Nobody can hear us," he said softly. "So tell me why we have to wait now that the ranchers' money is here."

"First, I'm in no mood to tangle with Usta's men to get that money down in Tom Nettles' safe. We've got to pick a time when we won't be hurried. Sometimes it takes a while to open one of those safes, even if it is a cracker box like that one of Tom's. And I don't intend to settle for just that money. Pettigrew has a fortune over there in his safe. He always keeps plenty of money there and that money the farmers brought in to pay for the dam is there, too."

Gumpy grinned, his eyes sparkling. "Yeah. We sure want to get that, too."

"Do you think we can just walk over and take it?"

"Of course not," Gumpy growled. "But when are we going to do it?"

"I've been thinking about it," Sitzman said. "We could work at night but there are too many disadvantages to that. I need light to see to open those safes. And somebody might see any light that leaked out to the street."

"You're not figuring on doing it in the daytime, are you?" Gumpy asked in disbelief.

"Exactly," Sitzman said.

He liked to show off his superior intelligence. But there were times when he wished Gumpy was quicker witted.

"How are you going to work that?" Gumpy asked.

"Tomorrow is the last day of school. There is going to be a program and picnic dinner at the school house. Nobody is going to miss that—except us."

Gumpy grinned. "That's when we're going to get the money?"

"Right," Sitzman said. "And just to make sure we have no trouble once we start, I've sent for the old gang."

Gumpy frowned. "What for? We don't want to share this money with them."

"Better to share it than not to get it at all," Sitzman said. "I've done a lot more thinking about this than you have. Things could get pretty sticky if Craig Usta gets wind of what we're doing. Do you want to face Ben Lozar or some of those other gun slicks he's brought in? Even if Klosson or Quill happened to stumble onto our plan, we'd have plenty of trouble. But with the old gang here, we can handle whatever comes up. And if we do get all the money in Nettles' safe and the bank, we'll have plenty for everyone."

"If we have all the gang, we don't need to wait till the school picnic," Gumpy said. "We can just raid the whole town any time."

"Half of us could get killed doing it that way," Sitzman said. "Don't you ever use your head? If we can clean out those safes and get out of town without anyone catching on, we'll have all the money without taking any risk."

Gumpy nodded. "Sure. But if we're going to be sneaky about it, why do we need all the boys?"

"I like to hedge my bets," Sitzman said.

"Can't we hedge our bet on this marshal and Hunch?" Gumpy asked worriedly. "I think they're getting suspicious. If they find out we're the ones who killed their fathers and got that money, they'd let the whole town know who we are."

Sitzman nodded. For once Gumpy was thinking straight. "Killing them wouldn't be much of a problem. But if we do it now, that would upset our plans to get this money. We've got to keep the lid on things till then. How suspicious are they?"

"Don't know," Gumpy admitted. "They act like

they're looking for something. You don't suppose they saw that watch of Matt Dekin's, do you? I left it on the bar when that skunky dog ran us out yesterday, you know."

Sitzman frowned. He had forgotten about that. "Could be," he said. "If they did, they know that somebody who was in this saloon then is the man who killed Matt Dekin and Pete Huckle. That could be what they are really looking for."

"What can we do?"

"Sit tight and keep our eyes open," Sitzman said. "I'm going down to Nettles and look over that safe. I think it will be an easy one to crack."

As he walked down to the store, he thought about Gumpy's carelessness in leaving Matt Dekin's watch on the bar yesterday. It wasn't likely that Dusty had seen it but there was always the chance. A good gambler never discounted such a possibility.

Usta's men were just leaving the grocery when Sitzman went in. He nodded to them then bought some crackers and cheese, looking over the safe back in the far corner. He'd seen safes like that. In fact, he'd opened a couple of them and he was sure he could get into this one in five minutes. The one over at the bank would be a bigger problem. But he'd never seen the safe he couldn't open if he had the time.

"Going to close for the school picnic tomorrow, I suppose," he said.

"Sure am," Nettles said. "Everybody is. Jennie is planning a big program."

"Bank won't close, will it?"

"I heard Mr. Pettigrew say he was going to that program," Nettles said. "There won't be a thing open in town."

Sitzman nodded and went back outside and returned to the saloon. Both the bank and the store would be closed and left unguarded tomorrow. His men were due to trickle in late this afternoon and tonight. He'd be ready.

As he went into the saloon, he met one of Usta's men coming out. There were no other customers in the saloon. He saw Gumpy waving to him to come to the bar. He hurried over. Maybe Gumpy had heard something important.

As Sitzman crowded close to hear what Gumpy had to say, Gumpy pulled his hands up from behind the bar. In one hand he held a wriggling garter snake. Sitzman gasped and fell back. If there was one thing in this world that he feared, it was a snake. Any snake. There was something about the wriggling things that sent a surge of horror through him.

He stumbled back until he hit a table and sank down in the chair beside it. For a moment, he thought he was going to heave up his dinner. Then he wondered if his heart was going to quit. He'd had a heart attack a little over a year ago and the doctor had warned him not to get too excited or work too hard. The work was no problem; he never intended to work hard again. But a scare like this was something else.

Gumpy came running around the end of the bar to

Sitzman. "I'm sorry," he babbled. "I didn't think about scaring you that bad. I just aimed to surprise you."

Sitzman sat very still as he felt his heart pounding. Was it going to quit? It was a terrifying fear for a moment. But after a minute, it began to quiet down. Then he glared up at Gumpy.

"If you ever do anything like that again, I'll kill you! I swear it! Do you understand?"

"Sure, sure," Gumpy said, backing off. "I knew you didn't like snakes. But I didn't think you'd turn up your toes if you saw one."

Gumpy went back behind the bar and Sitzman just sat there, letting his heart calm down. He wondered how close he had come to dying right then. His whole chest ached now. He'd rather face Ben Lozar over smoking guns than see another snake.

"You're worse about snakes than most women are about mice," Queeny said, pulling a chair up to Sitzman's table. "Can't stand them myself but I don't faint when I see one. I've been telling everyone I'm going to sing tonight. I figure we'll have a packed house."

"I hope so," Sitzman said. He didn't feel like talking to Queeny now but he had no choice. He didn't understand her. It didn't make sense that she'd come to Jawbone to make a living. There wasn't that much money to be had here unless she aimed to rob the bank. Maybe she did have her eye on the bank. He had seen her go into the bank this morning and spend quite a bit of time there. He wouldn't put anything past her, considering the way she had barged in here and hired herself to sing and cut herself in on the profits.

"Well, look who's here," Queeny said softly and pushed back her chair and got up.

Sitzman turned around and stared. He couldn't recall that Phoebus Pettigrew had ever come into the saloon since he and Gumpy had bought it. The banker stopped at one end of the bar and motioned with a finger to Queeny. She went over to him.

Sitzman wished he could hear what they were saying but when he started to get up, he discovered he was almost too weak to move. That scare had almost killed him, he decided. He still had a pain like a tightening band across his chest. He looked at Gumpy and Gumpy nodded, moving down the bar closer to the two, wiping off imaginary wet spots as he went.

Pettigrew didn't stay long and when he left, Queeny ordered Gumpy to bring her a drink. Sitzman got up then, feeling better. But his knees still threatened to buckle. He was convinced that another scare like the one he'd just had would kill him.

Stopping at the bar several feet from Queeny, he whispered to Gumpy. "Did you hear what they said?"

"Old Pettigrew asked Queeny to go for a buggy ride with him this evening." Gumpy whispered as if he couldn't believe it himself.

Sitzman nodded. Then there was something between the banker and Queeny. He'd give a great deal to know what it was. In fact, in view of his plans to relieve the bank of its overload in the vault tomorrow, he'd better find out. Queeny might have connections he didn't dream of. He'd known of gangs who had a woman as a front. Perhaps he and his men would have competition for that money in the bank.

Sitzman slid down the bar. "You have unusual friends," he said.

She smiled, staring at her glass. "So I do. Maybe I can get him to come and hear me sing tonight. He ought to be good for a real profit."

"He's not a regular customer here," Sitzman said, hoping she'd say more.

"I know," she said. "He's my customer, not yours."

He saw that he wasn't going to get anything from her without direct prying and he had Queeny pegged as one who would tell him nothing but lies if she thought he was prying. He went back to Gumpy as the doors banged open and Ben Lozar came in.

Gumpy moved off to serve Ben Lozar then came back to where Sitzman was standing as Dusty Deskin came in.

"That marshal is nosing around here too much," he whispered to Sitzman. "We've got to get rid of him."

"Just sit tight," Sitzman snapped. "Don't do something that will tip your hand."

Sitzman went back to the chair at the nearest table, his knees still weak. He saw Gumpy slide down the bar to talk to Ben Lozar. Dusty came over to him.

"Are you going to lock up for the school program tomorrow?" Dusty asked.

Sitzman shrugged. "Might as well. Everybody will

be up there, anyway. It seems to be the patriotic thing to do in this town. You'll be there, won't you?"

"Figure on it," Dusty said with a grin. "Might even help out with the program."

Sitzman didn't know whether to believe that or not. But he did believe that Dusty would be at the school house. He glanced at Gumpy. He was talking earnestly with Ben Lozar. Sitzman frowned. They were probably cooking up something that wouldn't be healthy for the marshal. Sitzman wasn't sure that was a wise thing to do right now.

XII

Dusty had followed Ben Lozar into the saloon to find out if there was any connection between the gunman and the two men who ran the saloon. Like Queeny, he was guessing that Serg Sitzman was the boss of the two men even though Sitzman insisted that Gumpy was the owner of the saloon and he just did the gambling.

As he left the saloon, he was still uncertain. Sitzman had practically ignored Lozar but Gumpy hadn't. The animated conversation that Gumpy and the gunman were having when Dusty left made Dusty more than a little suspicious.

Hunch had stayed outside to keep an eye on happenings there. He turned as Dusty came out.

"What did Lozar do?" he asked.

"He and Gumpy are talking like a couple of politicians," Dusty said. "What's going on out here?"

"Nothing much," Hunch said. "I just saw Ed Klosson and some of Wolfe's men. Don't know how long they've been in town. They either caught their horses or else came by Klosson's place and got some more. It appears to me that there could be a clash between those two outfits yet."

Dusty nodded. "That's always a possibility. Do you have any idea why Klosson came back to town instead of stopping at his place?"

"I think he might have a notion about guarding the bank to keep Usta's men from robbing it."

Dusty looked down toward the store, two doors south of the saloon. "I see a couple of Usta's men loafing there in front of the grocery. Could be they're guarding the ranchers' money."

"I reckon," Hunch said. "I guess there's nothing we can do about that."

"It's a good idea as long as it stays just like it is. Nobody's going to get hurt guarding his own stuff. It's when one of them decides to try to take what belongs to the other fellow that the fur will fly."

"What do we do now?"

"I want you to keep a sharp eye on Lozar and Gumpy," Dusty said. "I think I'll go up and see what we can do to help the teacher with her program tomorrow."

Hunch snorted. "You'd be safer down here facing Lozar."

Dusty grinned. "Maybe. But hot words don't burn like hot bullets."

Hunch turned and went into the saloon. Dusty crossed the street, stopping once to keep from being hit by a couple of boys dodging away from two others in some game they had started since leaving school. As he passed along the side of the bank, Vyrl Wolfe came to his office door and called Dusty inside.

"Know anything about a crazy donkey?" Wolfe asked.

Dusty looked at Wolfe in wide-eyed innocence. "Did you ever see a donkey that wasn't crazy?"

"My men reported seeing one out at the rocks where they planned to intercept that money shipment. This donkey was saddled with some kind of wild flopping blanket and went braying and bucking right into Usta's men. Scattered them all over the river bottom. That scared my boys' horses and they broke loose, leaving everybody afoot."

Dusty knew that Wolfe suspected him of creating that confusion with the donkey but he had no intention of admitting it. "Where did the donkey come from?" he asked.

"They didn't get a chance to find out," Wolfe admitted. "They were too busy trying to catch their horses. By the time they did, the donkey was gone and so was Usta and the money wagon." The contractor stared at Dusty. "Just thought you might know something about it. But that really wasn't what I called you in here for. One of my men just told me that he was down at Nettles' store and heard Usta say he'd given Ben Lozar orders to kill you."

There was something chilling about hearing it said

like that but Dusty wasn't surprised. "What was your man doing down at the store?" he asked as calmly as he could.

"Listening," Wolfe said frankly. "Now that Usta has the money to pay his gunmen, we want to know what he is going to have them do. Killing you seems to be the first order of business."

"I'll try to make that a hard job to do," Dusty said. "Thanks for the warning."

He went back outside and on up the street toward the school house. Jennie would still be there, cleaning up and getting ready for tomorrow's big day. It was no wonder those boys had been feeling so good. Except for the program and picnic dinner, school was over for this term.

Dusty rapped on the door jamb since the door was open. Jennie, busy inside with a broom, stopped and looked up.

"You!" she exclaimed. He thought for a moment she was going to throw the broom at him. "What do you want?"

"Invited inside, providing you don't use that broom on me," he said.

She frowned but finally nodded. "All right. Come in. I've got a lot of work to do." She began sweeping again with short violent strokes.

Dusty stepped inside. "Molly tells me you got the wrong idea about me and Queeny. She fell in the mud and—"

"I don't care the least bit what you and Queeny did,"

Jennie snapped. She swung the broom harder than ever.

"Maybe you don't care what happened," Dusty snapped back, "but I care what you think."

She stopped sweeping and stared at him in surprise.

"I came up here to see if you wanted Hunch to play his accordion for your program tomorrow," Dusty added quickly, realizing he'd said more than he had intended to.

"That would be wonderful," Jennie said meekly. "We have only one other number from the grown-ups. The children will do all the rest. Molly says this program usually includes some numbers from the parents."

Dusty grinned. "Hunch isn't exactly a parent but I'm sure he'll play for you."

"Will there be any trouble before tomorrow?" Jennie asked anxiously.

"I don't know," Dusty admitted. "There was almost a battle today but it was avoided. Things might stay calm for another day or two."

"Molly says the dam may not go in if the ranchers get their money here to pay their gun fighters."

"The money is in Nettles' store now," Dusty said. "But after tomorrow, you can get out of town and this war won't affect you."

"Oh, yes, it will," Jennie said. "I had some money my father left me in his will and Mr. Pettigrew talked me into investing it in the dam."

"That wasn't exactly a smart thing to do," Dusty said.

"It seemed smart enough at the time. There wasn't any talk of war then."

Dusty started to say something then stopped as he heard the distinct coo of a pigeon. "Are there pigeons in the attic here?"

Jennie shook her head. "They're homing pigeons. That's a project the boys had here at school. They've had those pigeons all winter. We often took them out a mile or so at noon and released them. They'd beat us back here every time."

Dusty nodded approvingly. "You were teaching them something besides what they found in books."

Hunch came puffing up to the door then. Dusty hurried outside.

"What's wrong, Hunch?"

"Could be nothing; could be real trouble," Hunch said. "Lozar and Gumpy left the saloon together. They seemed thicker than thieves. They said something about the school house, then went across the street toward the hardware store."

"Are they coming up here?" Jennie asked from the doorway.

"I doubt it," Hunch said. "I figure they're after Dusty and somebody must have told them that he came up here."

"You'd better go to the boarding house and stay there," Jennie said to Dusty.

Dusty shook his head. "That won't solve anything. Besides, Lozar has a room at the boarding house. I'd better find out right now what he's up to. Come on, Hunch."

"Wait a minute," Jennie said quickly. "I've got to

have some more colored paper for decorations for tomorrow's program. Mr. Nettles has some. I'll walk down town with you."

Dusty saw through that quickly. He couldn't allow it but it gave him a funny choked feeling. Just five minutes ago, Jennie had been ready to believe the worst of him. Now she was trying to protect him.

"I suppose you believe they won't shoot at me if you're along," he said. "You don't know Ben Lozar. If you think I'm going to let you get shot at, you're dead wrong."

"I'm going and you can't stop me," Jennie said. "This is a free country."

"That means I'm free to walk alone if I want to," Dusty said.

He turned toward town with Hunch falling in step with him. He was aware that Jennie had come out of the school house and shut the door and he heard her running feet as she tried to catch up. Suddenly her little dog, Napoleon, dashed past them. He had seen the direction Jennie was going and was racing ahead, glad of the opportunity to explore more worlds than just the area between the school house and the boarding house.

"Stay well behind me," Dusty said over his shoulder.

She evidently realized from his tone of voice that those words were an order not to be challenged. She slowed her pace. Dusty and Hunch went on, Dusty's eyes searching every corner that could hide a man. It didn't make sense that Lozar would try an ambush but, now that Usta had the money to buy the allegiance of the gunmen, there was no predicting what his orders might be.

Pettigrew had a little stable behind the bank where he kept his high stepping blood bay and his one-horse cart. Farther down the alley, behind the hardware, Fred Yoeman had a small stable, too. His house was across the alley from the hardware store so the stable was handy to both his store and his house.

"Maybe we'd ought to check out those barns," Dusty said softly.

He started to turn off the street toward Pettigrew's barn when Napoleon began yapping excitedly up at Yoeman's barn. Dusty caught Hunch's arm and stopped him.

"Maybe another skunk," Hunch said uneasily.

"Does he usually bark at these barns?" Dusty asked over his shoulder without taking his eyes off the barn.

"No," Jennie said. "He always runs around them but he never barks."

"Something's wrong," Hunch said. "Let's—"

Dusty suddenly grabbed Hunch and jerked him down as he saw some movement at the door of Yoeman's barn. A shot split the quiet of the town but the bullet snapped harmlessly over Dusty's head.

Rolling like a weed in a high wind, Dusty got behind the corner of Pettigrew's barn. He didn't have a gun and for a moment, he almost wished he hadn't promised himself never to use a gun. Being shot at could change a man's outlook on life.

Another bullet nicked the corner of the barn only inches from Dusty's head, reminding him that he was pinned down here with no way of fighting back.

XIII

Dusty saw that Hunch was staying right where he was, lying flat in a little depression. Dusty was sure that the ambusher was after him so Hunch was probably safe, anyway. Jennie was protected by Pettigrew's barn from any stray shots.

After those two shots, however, there were no more. Dusty peeked around the corner. Nothing was moving up at Yoeman's barn, which was no more than half a block away. Those shots should soon attract a crowd. Perhaps the ambusher had decided not to wait for the privilege of identifying himself.

Suddenly a man exploded from the door of the barn and sprinted toward the rear of the hardware store. At the same instant, Dusty saw a man dodging around the rear corner of the restaurant farther up the alley. He guessed that there had been two bushwhackers. He ran after the man heading for the hardware store.

"That may be a trick," Hunch shouted from his prone position.

Dusty didn't stop; he was in the open now, anyway. No shot came from the barn and he gained quickly on the fleeing man. He was at the corner of the hardware store before he recognized Gumpy Alvis, half way along the side of the store.

The bartender had obviously been spending too much time behind his bar and not enough exercising. He wasn't much of a runner. Before Gumpy reached the street, Dusty had almost caught him. Gumpy suddenly stopped and turned, holding up his hands.

"I don't have a gun," he said.

"What did you do with it?" Dusty demanded, grabbing Gumpy's arm.

"I left it in the barn," Gumpy whimpered. "I didn't shoot at you, anyway."

"Who did? Ben Lozar?"

Gumpy nodded. "He's ashamed because he missed. He says next time he'll face you in the street."

Dusty shoved Gumpy toward the street. "Let's go."

"Where?" Gumpy asked.

"To jail."

"What for? I told you I didn't shoot at you."

"You helped Lozar plan the ambush. That makes you guilty, too."

"You're not going to put me in Zeke Torberg's jail, are you?" he asked suddenly, stopping short on the walk between the hardware store and the land office.

"Only jail in town," Dusty said.

"I'm not going," Gumpy snapped.

Dusty pinched Gumpy's arm till he winced. "You're going. What's wrong with Torberg's jail?"

"It ain't his jail; it's him," Gumpy said. But then he clamped his mouth shut and refused to say any more.

Dusty pushed Gumpy across the street and into the

deputy's office. Torberg was slumped at his desk, a half full bottle in front of him.

"I told you, you can't use my jail," Torberg said as Dusty pushed Gumpy toward a cell. "And you sure can't put him in there."

"Have the town build me a jail and I won't use yours," Dusty said.

Dusty slammed the door behind Gumpy then leaned against the bars. "Where did Lozar go?"

"I didn't ask him where he was going," Gumpy said, scowling. Suddenly his face brightened. "You might look in the saloon. He'd like to have you try to arrest him."

Dusty knew that he should put Lozar behind bars. He had a good reason now. Then he looked over at Zeke Torberg, already far gone in that bottle. It wouldn't do any good to arrest Lozar, even if he could. Torberg and Usta would let him out just like they had before.

Dusty thought of his suspicion of Gumpy after that watch had disappeared so quickly from the bar yesterday. He turned back to the cell.

"Where were you before you came to Jawbone, Gumpy?" he asked.

"That's none of your business," Gumpy said sullenly.

"I'm making it my business. Were you ever in Kansas?"

Gumpy scowled and shook his head. "Colorado and Oklahoma."

Dusty didn't believe him but he didn't know how to

force him to tell the truth without going into the cell and using his fists. That wasn't Dusty's way.

While he was debating about ways of loosening Gumpy's tongue, Torberg got up from his chair and staggered over to the cell.

"I'm glad you're in there, you scum," he snarled at Gumpy. "You're going to cough up my money."

Gumpy backed away from the bars. "I didn't take your money," he said.

"That gambler of yours did," Torberg said. "You own the place so you can make up what I lost."

Dusty saw the fear of death in Gumpy's eyes. Maybe it was because the deputy was drunk or maybe he had other reasons. Either way, Dusty saw an opportunity and he never turned down an opening like this.

"Somebody cheat you, Torberg?" he asked.

The deputy nodded. "That sneaking gambler over at the saloon. He dealt from the bottom of the deck."

"How much did you lose?" Dusty pressed.

"Everything I had." Torberg gripped the bars and glared at Gumpy. "You're going to pay me back every cent of that. Do you hear?"

"Talk to Serg about it," Gumpy said from the far wall of the cell.

"I'm talking to you," Torberg said.

"Maybe you need another drink," Dusty suggested.

"Yeah, maybe I do," the deputy agreed and staggered back to his desk, which was out of sight of the cell where Gumpy was locked in.

Dusty moved over out of sight of Gumpy, too, and

poured the deputy's glass full and handed it to him. He slumped into his chair and grabbed the glass like a thirsty man who had just escaped from the desert. Dusty prodded Torberg about the money he had lost.

"You know Sitzman will never give back your money," he said.

"He'd better or I'll kill him."

"Maybe it would be easier to get it from Gumpy."

Torberg nodded and poured his glass full again. "I'll take it out of Gumpy's hide."

"What if he won't give you your money?"

Torberg half reared out of his chair. "I'll kill him with my bare hands," he roared.

Dusty stole a glance around the corner at Gumpy in his cell. He was squatting on the edge of the bunk and his face was a pasty gray. Dusty couldn't really blame Gumpy for being afraid of Torberg. Right now, Torberg was so far gone on the whiskey that he would hardly be capable of rational action.

"Maybe he doesn't have that much money with him," Dusty said.

Torberg's voice was so slurred, it was hard to distinguish his words. "If he ain't got the money, I'll kill him."

Dusty reached over and eased Torberg back into his chair then pushed the bottle and glass aside and let him lay his head on the desk. He was beyond doing anything for himself now.

"Now wait a minute, Zeke," Dusty said. "Killing Gumpy won't get your money. Let me talk to him for you."

Dusty shoved a chair around as though he were struggling with someone.

"Now you just sit there till I talk to him. If I can't get the money out of him, I'll let you in his cell."

He stepped around the corner toward Gumpy's cell. Gumpy was backed against the far wall and actually looked relieved when Dusty appeared.

"Don't let him in here, Dusty," he begged.

"It's hard to keep him out," Dusty said.

"Let me out. I swear I'll come back as soon as he's sober."

Dusty paused as though considering. "I might let you out and even drop the charges against you if you'll tell me what I want to know."

Gumpy shot a fearful glance at the corner where he evidently expected Torberg to appear any second. "All right," he agreed. "What do you want to know? And hurry before he gets tired of waiting."

"I want to know what you and Sitzman are doing in Jawbone."

"We're running a saloon," Gumpy said quickly. "We ain't mixed up in this fight over the dam. But I can tell you that Ben Lozar has orders to kill you. The ranchers are not going to let that dam be built."

"Killing me won't stop it," Dusty said.

"They figure that's the first step. You've snarled up their plans more than once already."

"Since you know so much about their plans, you and Sitzman must be siding with them," Dusty said.

"No, we're not," Gumpy denied. "We have customers from both sides and we aim to keep it that way."

"You and Sitzman are up to something," Dusty said, watching Gumpy's face. The startled look in his eyes told Dusty he'd hit the target.

"No, we ain't," Gumpy denied emphatically. "We're just tending to our own business."

Dusty nodded. "That business is what I want to find out about. What is it?"

Gumpy frowned but he didn't answer. He had hedged as long as he could. He wasn't going to tell any more. Dusty started to turn away.

"Hey!" Gumpy yelled. "You said you'd turn me loose if I told you everything."

"That's right," Dusty said. "And I'll do it if you'll tell me everything."

"I did," Gumpy shouted.

"That's a lie and you know it, Gumpy," Dusty said. "When you decide to tell me exactly what you and Sitzman are doing here, then I'll turn you loose."

Gumpy pinched his lips together. His fear of Torberg was wearing down a little since he hadn't heard anything from him for a while. Perhaps he suspected that Torberg had passed out from his whiskey.

Dusty sighed. He wasn't going to get any more out of Gumpy. But he wasn't going to turn him loose, either. He hadn't told him a thing that he hadn't already known or suspected.

"I'll come back later," Dusty said. "If Torberg has left you alive that long, maybe you'll be ready to tell me the rest."

Gumpy swore, almost sobbing in his fright, but he didn't say any more. Dusty decided that his fear of Sitzman might be even greater than it was of Torberg. Or perhaps Gumpy was the man Dusty was looking for. In that case, he couldn't blame Gumpy for not telling. Dusty's own revenge might be worse than anything either Torberg or Sitzman would do.

A shadow fell on the window and Dusty looked up to see Serg Sitzman going by, heading south. Sitzman glanced in but he didn't stop. He probably didn't suspect that Gumpy was locked in a cell here.

XIV

Serg Sitzman saw Dusty in the deputy's office as he went past. He also saw Zeke Torberg slumped over at his desk. He guessed that Torberg had emptied that bottle of whiskey he'd given him when he'd cleaned him out of his money at the gambling table.

If he had time, he'd stop and find out what Dusty was doing in the deputy's office. Maybe he had put Gumpy in jail. Gumpy had left a few minutes ago with Ben Lozar and there had been some shooting over behind the hardware store. Normally, Sitzman would have looked into that but he had other things on his mind now.

He had just seen a rider mosey into town on the river road and stop at the livery barn. It was time for Sitzman's men to begin drifting into town and he figured Hollohan would be the first. He wanted to talk to

140

Hollohan before the gunman had a chance to wander over town.

He turned in at the barn. Tall, lanky Hollohan was there with the livery man, unsaddling his horse. He glanced up at Sitzman but gave no sign of recognition.

"Howdy, stranger," Sitzman said. "Figuring on staying in town long?"

"Overnight, maybe," Hollohan said.

"I was just telling him that the only place to stay is Molly's boarding house," the barn owner said. "I hear she's full."

"I've slept in haymows before," Hollohan said.

The livery man went into his office and Sitzman moved closer to Hollohan. "The rest of the boys out there?" he asked softly.

"Yeah," Hollohan said. "I came on in to make sure there hadn't been any change in plans."

"There hasn't," Sitzman said. "Except that there are two safes to crack instead of one."

Hollohan whistled under his breath. "Should be a nice haul."

"It will be," Sitzman said. "I want you to stay around the barn here. When the other fellows come in, keep them out of sight. Don't let more than one or two come up to the saloon for a drink. Strangers are noticeable in a little town like this and we don't want to rouse too much attention."

"Carl will be the next one in if I don't go back and tell them the deal is off. I'll send him back to tell the others to slip in without letting anyone see them."

"Good," Sitzman said. "I'll check with you later."

"When do we do it?"

"Tomorrow during the last hour of school picnic. Nobody will be down here in town then."

Sitzman went back outside and started up the street. He saw Pettigrew go out the back door of the bank and into the little barn on the alley. He remembered Pettigrew's invitation to take Queeny for a ride this evening. Maybe he had changed his mind and decided to take her this afternoon. Sitzman frowned. He hoped not. He'd been trying to think of a way to eavesdrop on those two and he wouldn't have a chance unless it was dark.

He'd give plenty to know what the connection was between Queeny and the banker. As crazy as it seemed, he had the feeling that Queeny might just get away with the bank's money before he could get his own hands on it.

Sitzman saw Pettigrew come out of the little barn and head for home. Maybe he had harnessed his horse to have him ready for his evening ride. Or maybe he had even considered going after Queeny now but had decided to wait until dark because of his reputation. Tongues would wag if the banker took another woman, especially one like Queeny, for a ride. After dark, the banker might not be discovered in his little escapade.

Sitzman turned into the deputy's office on his way back to the saloon. Torberg was still slumped over his desk, out like a light. Dusty was not in sight. He saw Gumpy back in one of the cells.

"What are you doing in there?" Sitzman demanded.

"Dusty put me here," Gumpy admitted. "Caught me after Lozar tried to ambush him and missed."

"Didn't think Lozar ever missed," Sitzman said. "He's always bragging that he doesn't botch up his jobs."

"He botched this one," Gumpy said as Sitzman went to the desk and got the key to the cell without disturbing Torberg.

"Did Dusty think you shot at him?" Sitzman asked as he unlocked the door.

"He figured it was Lozar, although I don't know how he knew we were together." Gumpy looked over at Torberg sleeping off his whiskey. "The dirty rat!" he snorted.

"He just drank too much."

Gumpy nodded. "He was threatening to kill me if I didn't give him back the money you won from him. Dusty had me thinking Zeke was ready to come into the cell after me and he promised to let me out if I'd tell him what he wanted to know."

"What did you say?" Sitzman demanded, grabbing Gumpy's arm.

"Nothing that he didn't already know. But he's suspicious, Serg. He asked me if I'd ever been in Kansas."

Sitzman led Gumpy out of the deputy's office and on to the saloon. "Maybe we can't wait till we clean out the town to take care of him," he said.

The saloon was practically empty. Ben Lozar was

143

behind the bar where Sitzman had left him while he went down to the livery barn. Gumpy took his place now.

"Watch for any of the boys who come in," Sitzman said softly to Gumpy. "Maybe you can bed them down in the back room. The rest will have to sleep wherever they can."

Gumpy nodded and Sitzman went to the front window to watch the town. The sun was low and the businesses were closing for the day. The bank had been closed for some time now.

As twilight settled in, Sitzman saw Pettigrew come down the street and go back of the bank toward the little barn. He'd be getting his cart now and going after Queeny. Sitzman went out on the street. He saw two riders down along the river. But they went past town and turned in behind the barn. That would be two more of his men. There would be ten when they all got here. They were all good with a gun. Not even Usta's gun hands would dare to go up against them.

Moving down the street past the grocery to a spot where he could see the barn behind the bank, he watched Pettigrew get his horse and cart out of the little barn. He had seen Pettigrew driving the cart a few times. It was a one-horse rig with just two wheels. Pettigrew had taken a top from a buggy and put it on the cart. That top offered both protection from the weather and privacy.

Sitzman thought that Pettigrew might drive up to the boarding house to get Queeny but he merely swung the cart around and hitched the horse to one corner of the barn. Apparently he didn't want anyone to see him calling for Queeny.

Pettigrew did walk up toward the boarding house and Sitzman crossed the street to the bank where he could get a better view of the two when they came back to the cart. He stopped beside the bank as he saw Dusty go down the alley to the cart. Dusty stood beside Pettigrew's horse for a while doing something but from this distance, Sitzman couldn't even guess what it was.

Dusty went on and was out of sight before Pettigrew showed up again. Pettigrew apparently hadn't gone far but he must have given some signal because it was only a couple of minutes until Queeny came down the alley to the cart.

Sitzman slipped down the alley-way beside the bank to the barn. He had an idea and he put it into action the minute Pettigrew had untied his hose and climbed into the cart with Queeny. Running to the cart, Sitzman caught the back of it as the high stepping horse started off across the vacant lot behind the feed store toward the river.

Clinging to the rear of the cart, Sitzman found a place to put his feet on the axle of the cart. He was within a couple of feet of the two riding in the cart seat but they would never suspect that he was there.

"I hope nobody saw you leave the boarding house," Pettigrew said, worriedly.

"I don't think they did," Queeny said. "What did you want to see me about?"

"We'll discuss it when we get out of town," Pettigrew said and slapped the reins on the horse.

"I suppose it wouldn't help your reputation as an upstanding banker to be seen riding around with me," Queeny said disgustedly. "Watch the bumps, Phoeby. This cart doesn't have any springs."

"It has good springs," Pettigrew argued. "We've just got too big a load."

"Well, don't look at me when you say that," Queeny said testily.

Sitzman agreed with Queeny about the rough ride. But the cart hadn't been built to haul three people, especially one his size hanging on the rear. He wished they'd get to a place Pettigrew felt it was safe to stop. His position was getting mighty uncomfortable.

They came to the river with barely a word being said in the cart. The horse plunged into the edge of the water to get a drink. Apparently Pettigrew hadn't watered him before starting.

"I've been in this creek once today," Queeny complained. "Let's get out of here."

Pettigrew pulled the horse around and started him straight up the bank to the road. It was then that it happened. Sitzman had no idea what caused the bellyband on the harness to break but it did and the shafts shot up in the air. The cart tipped over backward right into the edge of the river.

Sitzman, hanging on the back, was on the bottom of the pile. He heard Pettigrew curse and Queeny scream then he was pushed down into the mud and water by

146

the cart top with Pettigrew and Queeny on it.

Sitzman clawed his way out from under the cart, splashing water and mud wildly in his attempt to keep from drowning. He realized he was hitting someone as he flailed around but his only concern was to get his head above water. When he did, he saw that he was ten feet from the river bank and Pettigrew and Queeny were there with him.

Queeny was the first to get her breath. "You stinking spy!" she screamed at him. "Your weight was what caused this." She swung a fist at Sitzman that barely missed.

"I'll have you arrested!" Pettigrew yelled. "You had no business on that cart."

Sitzman was catching his breath after his dunking. "Just what business did you have taking Queeny for a ride? I'm sure your wife will be glad to hear all about it."

"Don't you dare tell her," Pettigrew said, his anger suddenly turning to pleading.

"I'll have your hide for dumping us in the river," Queeny shouted.

Sitzman started to say that Dusty was to blame for it all. But he knew they'd just call that an excuse. Sitzman realized now that Dusty might have cut that bellyband almost in two, figuring on disrupting Pettigrew's evening ride. Evidently Dusty didn't trust Pettigrew, either. That bellyband would have broken somewhere before the cart got back to town. Sitzman's added weight had caused it to happen the first time any extra strain had been put on it.

Sitzman scrambled out of the river and headed for town on foot. He wouldn't overhear any of Pettigrew's and Queeny's conversation now. They were both sputtering as they climbed out of the water and Pettigrew led the horse with the broken harness back to town, dragging the cart behind.

By the time he got back to town, Sitzman had begun to dry off. He saw Dusty on the street near the deputy's office and it reminded him that Dusty was getting too suspicious. Gumpy wanted to get rid of him. Maybe they'd better do it tonight.

Going in the back door of the saloon, he called Gumpy from behind the bar. "Get someone to tend bar for you," he said softly. "We're going to get rid of Dusty."

"Sure will," Gumpy said eagerly.

Sitzman found the big skinning knife he kept in the back of the saloon and stuck it in his belt. When Gumpy showed up, they went out the back door together.

"What's the plan?" Gumpy asked. "We can't tackle him on the street. He's too smart to be caught by surprise there."

Sitzman nodded. "You're right. But when he goes to the boarding house for the night, he'll be relaxed. We'll hit him then."

"Sounds good," Gumpy agreed.

"You'll hide by the door and you'll use this." He handed Gumpy the knife.

Gumpy took it reluctantly. "I don't like a knife."

"If you use a gun there, everybody in the boarding house will look out and see you. Do you want that?"

Gumpy shook his head. "Of course not. I can handle one of these, all right."

Sitzman led the way down the dark side street to the boarding house. They had to plan this perfectly. Dusty had an uncanny way of turning things around.

"You'll hide behind that puny little bush Molly has growing to the right of the door," Sitzman said softly as they approached the house. "I'll be close by in case you have any trouble. But there isn't room there for both of us."

"How close will you be?" Gumpy asked suspiciously.

"I'll—"

Sitzman broke off as Molly came around the corner of the house from the shed, carrying an armload of firewood. It was pretty dark but not dark enough to hide them from her sharp eyes.

"What are you two doing here?" she demanded.

"We wanted to see if Queeny was coming down to the saloon tonight," Sitzman said quickly. "She promised to sing there."

"She just came in looking like a drowned rat," Molly snorted. "That's twice in one day. You wouldn't want her singing the way she's cussing now."

"We'll wait at the saloon for her to come," Sitzman said and turned back toward town with Gumpy.

When Molly had gone into the house, Sitzman stopped and breathed a sigh of relief. "Never thought she'd be outside this time of night. Now you get behind that bush. Dusty should be coming any time now."

Sitzman went to the far corner of the house after making sure Gumpy was hidden from anyone approaching the door. Sitzman doubted if he had nerve enough himself to jab a knife into a man but Gumpy did. He had an instinct for killing.

Sitzman guessed he had been waiting about ten minutes when he heard someone coming. He peered through the darkness and made out two men before he could recognize either one. He cursed softly. He should have known Dusty would have his sidekick, Hunch, with him. But then he and Gumpy wanted to get rid of Hunch, too. It was his money they had stolen when they'd killed Matt Dekin and Pete Huckle.

He switched his eyes to Gumpy. He was ready and he wouldn't hesitate because there were two of them. They came toward the door and for once, Sitzman realized, Dusty wasn't suspicious.

But just as Dusty was almost close enough for Gumpy to leap to the attack, the porch door banged open and Molly heaved out a dishpan full of hot water. The water hit the bush full force and Gumpy screamed as the hot water sloshed over him.

XV

Dusty was as surprised as Gumpy when Molly threw the hot water on the bush. Gumpy roared as he fell back, dropping the knife. The blade of the knife caught a faint glint from the light filtering out of the parlor window. Dusty leaped toward Gumpy, slapping a foot down on the knife before Gumpy could recover from the hot bath.

"Who did you aim to stab?" Dusty demanded.

"That's a silly question," Molly said, coming down from the porch. "He was laying for you. That gambler, Sitzman, was with him earlier."

"I'm scalded," Gumpy wailed. "Ain't you going to do nothing for me?"

"I might cut off a roast if you're done enough," Molly said. "Come here. Let's see how good a job I did."

"Where's Sitzman?" Dusty asked.

"I don't know," Gumpy whimpered. "I'm burned."

"Not very bad," Molly said disgustedly after looking at Gumpy. "Go on back to the saloon and pour some whiskey on your burns."

Gumpy turned and ran before Dusty vetoed Molly's leniency. Dusty let him go then turned to Molly. "How did you know he was there?"

Molly chuckled. "I saw him and Sitzman hanging around here earlier so, after I went in the house, I peeked out the window. Sure enough, they sneaked back and Gumpy hid behind that bush. I figured what he was up to so I put this pan of water on the stove and really stuffed the firebox full of wood."

"That wasn't dishwater?" Hunch asked.

"You wouldn't catch me putting my hands in water that hot. Soon as I heard you coming, I got the pan of water and sneaked out to the door. Then when I figured you was about as close as I dared let you get, I dumped that water on the bush. Don't reckon it will help the bush any but it sure flushed Gumpy out."

"I've been getting suspicious of those two," Dusty said. "I've seen Sitzman sizing up the safe in Nettles' store and also looking over the bank."

"Think he's fixing to rob them?" Molly asked.

"Wouldn't surprise me," Dusty said.

"That's why they wanted to get rid of you," she concluded. "They figured you were getting wise to them."

"Maybe," Dusty agreed "I've seen some shady characters riding into town this afternoon. I recognized a couple of them. Real tough gun hands."

"What's Sitzman and Gumpy have to do with them?" Molly asked.

"Maybe nothing; maybe a lot," Dusty said. "What do you know about Serg Sitzman, anyway? Where did he come from?"

"Let's go into the kitchen," Molly said. "I feel like a fool standing out here in the yard with this empty dishpan in my hand."

Dusty and Hunch followed Molly inside. "I don't know too much about him," she said, her voice softer now. "He and Gumpy came here together and Gumpy bought the saloon. Sitzman began gambling there. They're mighty closed mouthed about where they've been or what they've done."

"They may have a good reason for that," Dusty said. "Ever hear either one of them mention Kansas?"

Molly shook her head. "Never heard either one mention any place they'd been. I figure that's against their rules. Now if there's nothing else you want from me, I'll get started on setting some dough for light biscuits for breakfast."

Dusty grinned. "Wouldn't want to keep you from that. Thanks for the hot shower you gave Gumpy. That saved me from getting carved up."

"Don't mention it. Just be here for breakfast in the morning. A cook don't take kindly to these late breakfasts."

Dusty went back out on the porch instead of into the parlor. He wanted to talk to Hunch in private.

"Do you figure Sitzman and Gumpy are the two we're looking for?" he asked once they were alone.

"Mighty hard not to suspect them," Hunch said. "They could have used my money to buy that saloon."

"If we can prove they're the ones, we'll get your money back if we have to take it out of their hides. I have a feeling those tough hands drifting into town may be part of Sitzman's gang."

"Think they'll try to crack those safes tonight?"

Dusty considered that a moment. "I doubt it. If they were going to try to open the safes at night, they wouldn't need all those men. Sounds to me more like they were planning to do it in daylight. They might try to be sneaky but if they get caught, they'll have enough men to pull it off, anyway."

"How about tomorrow during the school program?" Hunch suggested.

"Exactly what I was thinking," Dusty agreed. "Almost everybody will be at that program, according to Jennie."

"If they figure on robbing both places, then they must not be helping Usta, either."

"I don't figure they're helping anybody except themselves," Dusty said. "Now I've already promised Jennie you'd play your accordion at the program. Maybe I can keep an eye on the town."

"I'd better go in and find out how many pieces she wants me to play," Hunch said.

He started through the door but Dusty caught his sleeve. "Hold it, Hunch. I hear some horses coming. Why would they come here instead of the livery stable?"

Dusty and Hunch stepped off the porch and backed against the wall. The horses came closer until they stopped only a few yards from the door. It wasn't until the two riders swung down that Dusty recognized one as Vyrl Wolfe.

"Who have you got with you?" Dusty asked, stepping out from the shadows.

"A Big U cowboy we caught sneaking around our construction camp," Wolfe said. "He's got quite a story to tell. I wanted you to hear it."

"Better bring him in where there is some light," Dusty suggested and opened the door. Wolfe led his prisoner across the porch and into the light of the kitchen. Molly motioned them on into the living room and followed them in.

"Anybody know this jasper?" Wolfe asked.

Dusty looked at the cowboy. He showed some bruises on his face and his pants were torn. He guessed he had been treated pretty rough to loosen his tongue.

"He admits he's a Big U rider and he is forking a Big U horse," Wolfe said.

"What was he doing at your construction camp?" Dusty asked.

"We had to use a little persuasion to find that out ourselves," Wolfe admitted. "But his tongue finally got unglued and he told us he'd been sent to spy us out. They're figuring on paying us a visit tonight and wipe out our camp."

"Your men are armed, ain't they?" Molly asked.

"Sure," Wolfe said. "We're ready to fight a war. But not the way Usta plans to fight it. We're camped down in that little draw right close to where we aim to start work on the dam. Usta figures on stampeding about three hundred big steers down that canyon tonight at midnight. At least, that's what this fellow says."

Dusty whistled softly. "That sure would wipe you out. You'd be lucky to save your necks."

"I doubt if anybody would get killed," Wolfe said. "But that stampede would ruin all of our equipment. It would cost a fortune to replace it and we couldn't get it in time to build the dam this summer."

"A sneaky scheme," Molly said. "What are you going to do about it?"

She was looking straight at Dusty and so were Wolfe and Hunch. Dusty spoke to Wolfe. "How long would it take you to move your equipment out of the little draw?"

"Quite a while even in daylight," Wolfe said. "We'd smash a lot of it trying to get it out at night."

"We've got to do something," Dusty said. "Come on. Let's get out there. We'll think of something."

"What about this cowboy?"

"Bring him along. We might tie him up right in the middle of camp. He should enjoy seeing his buddies come charging in."

The cowboy's eyes widened but he held his tongue. Dusty ran out the door with Hunch right behind him. Wolfe brought out the cowboy.

"Are most of your men out there?" Dusty asked.

"All of them are," Wolfe said.

Dusty didn't waste any more time. He headed for the livery barn on the run, leaving Hunch to bring up the rear. Hunch couldn't move very fast but Dusty knew he'd be there by the time Dusty had their horses caught out of the corral behind the livery barn.

The livery man helped Dusty get the horses in. Dusty noticed several extra horses in the corral, but there were no extra men in sight and he didn't have time to ask the stable man about them. Dusty and Hunch saddled up quickly. Outside, they met Wolfe with his prisoner and they kicked their horses into a gallop up the river toward the construction camp.

Dusty mulled the problem over as they rode and had a plan by the time they pulled their horses to a halt at the edge of camp. He saw that every man was wide awake and waiting for Wolfe to return.

"What do we do?" Wolfe asked Dusty expectantly.

"Get some of your dynamite," Dusty said. "We'll plant charges of dynamite up the draw from camp. You've got men who can set it off at just the right time, haven't you?"

"Sure have," Wolfe said eagerly. "I won't have men working for me who can't handle dynamite."

Dusty marked the spots, five of them, across the draw above the camp and Wolfe's men set the dynamite and strung the fuses.

He watched the men work hurriedly. They were as excited over the prospects of the surprise due the cowboys as Dusty was. But Dusty was worried, too. There was the possibility that the captured cowboy had lied or he might have been wrong in the time set for the stampede.

The five sets of dynamite were ready an hour before midnight. Wolfe assigned a man to light each of the five fuses. The fuses were necessarily long. Timing was going to be very important.

"They know how long it will take each fuse to reach the dynamite," Wolfe assured Dusty. "If they can just

157

judge how close the cattle are, those sticks will blow up right in their faces."

There was nothing to do but wait and Dusty found that was by far the hardest part of it. What if this was just a false alarm to get him and Hunch out of town? Maybe midnight was the time set to break into the bank and Nettles' store and rob those safes. Perhaps this cowboy was actually one of a gang of outlaws and letting him get caught so he could tell this wild tale about a stampede to wipe out the construction camp was just part of the plot to get Dusty and Hunch out of the way.

Midnight neared and everything around the camp remained peaceful. Dusty found it hard to quiet his suspicions that they had been tricked. But if they had, there wasn't anything he could do about it now. The outlaws who had sifted into town during the afternoon and evening had had plenty of time now to do whatever they might have planned to do.

Midnight came and there was no sound up the draw. Men around Dusty tensed, waiting, listening.

"Suppose it's a false alarm?" Wolfe asked.

The camp fire had been allowed to die down so Dusty couldn't see the face of the captured cowboy but he could imagine the smirk that must be on it if this was a trick.

Then suddenly Dusty caught a sound and he touched Wolfe's arm.

"Listen."

The contractor cocked an ear then muttered, "Thunder?"

158

"Stampede," Dusty corrected. "Tell your men to be ready with those matches."

It was almost a relief to Dusty to hear that stampede coming. This whole thing wasn't a trick. Earlier, he had placed the men with guns in a semi-circle a few yards above the camp to try to split the stampede around the camp in case the steers got past the dynamite blasts. Dusty wasn't sure that the men could time their explosions right. If they were late, the cattle would be past the dynamite before it blew up.

"How long are the fuses?" Dusty asked.

"About a minute," Wolfe said.

"Tell them to light the fuses," Dusty said, guessing at the time it would take the cattle to reach the dynamite. They were coming fast. He could hear the cowboys yelling behind them, whipping them into a frenzy. They would be hard to stop, even with dynamite.

Wolfe yelled at his men to light the fuses. Dusty saw the little sparks at the advance spots.

With the fuses sputtering and the stampede bearing down on the camp in a thundering wave, the men waited.

XVI

Even in the dim light, the flow of the stampede was visible as it came around a bend in the draw a couple of hundred yards ahead. Dusty heard the yelling of the cowboys above the roar of thundering hoofs and they added a few shots fired in the air to drive the frenzied cattle faster toward the camp. The men who had lit the dynamite fuses came running back to the others.

"How long?" Dusty asked.

"Any second now," one of the men said.

It seemed to Dusty that the cattle were almost on the line where the dynamite had been set. But still there were no explosions.

Then suddenly the charge in the center erupted with an orange burst and a deafening roar. Before that had died, the charges to the right and left ripped the night apart. Above the roar of the stampede now came the terrified bawling of the cattle closest to those explosions. Dusty thought that some of them might have been caught in the blasts.

For a minute there was utter confusion where the charges had gone off. The men at the camp waited tensely, their guns ready. Then the yelling of the cowboys changed to alarm and Dusty guessed that the lead steers had turned around, reversing the momentum, and the whole herd was now stampeding back the way it had come. Dusty knew the cowboys would never be able to stop it. They'd have all they could do to get out of the way.

"I guess that puts an end to that," Dusty said.

"Your idea saved the camp," Wolfe said thankfully. "What do we do with this cowboy?"

Dusty considered. "No use putting him in jail in town. Usta and Torberg would just let him out. He's done his good turn for us. Why don't you turn him loose and let him try to explain to Usta how we happened to be ready for his stampede?"

"Good idea," Wolfe agreed. "I'd like to hear the story he'll cook up to tell Craig Usta. Are you heading back for town tonight, Dusty?"

"Right now," Dusty said. "I think the bank and Nettles's store are marked for a hold-up. I saw several tough hands drifting into town this afternoon. They didn't come for the school picnic."

Wolfe nodded. "How could they have heard about all that money being in town?"

"I'd guess from Sitzman or Gumpy," Dusty said. "They know everything that is going on."

"If those farmers lose that money in Pettigrew's bank, this construction project will end before it begins. Isn't there anything we can do?"

"I think maybe there is," Dusty said. "I have the feeling that enough gunmen rode in this afternoon to tree the whole town. But if that money wasn't in the bank when they hit, they'd have a hard time stealing it."

"You mean we should take the money out of the bank and hide it?"

"Exactly," Dusty nodded. "We surely can find some safe place to hide it. I'm certain it will be safer that way than it will be in Pettigrew's vault. A good safe cracker can open that."

"Just how are you going to convince Pettigrew to go along with that idea?" Wolfe asked.

"That will be your problem," Dusty said. "You are

the one who will lose your job if something happens to that money. Pettigrew should listen to you."

"Where can we put it if we get it out of the bank?" Wolfe asked.

"I was thinking of Fred Yoeman's hardware store," Dusty said. "His back room is used mostly for a place to make coffins, I understand. Nobody would think of looking there."

"Sounds good," Wolfe agreed. "I'll stay there and guard it. But they may miss me at the program and picnic tomorrow. I've already told Jennie I'd be there."

Dusty turned that over in his mind for a minute. "Can your men keep a secret?"

"There's not a loose tongue among them."

"All right. We'll tell everybody that you got killed tonight. Either by the stampede or the dynamite."

Wolfe nodded. "Let's make it the stampede. It might make the ranchers feel a little guilty. What if somebody wants to come in and see the body?"

"We'll let Fred Yoeman figure a way to keep them out," Dusty grinned. "You'll be right where they'll expect you to be—in the back of the hardware store. Of course, you'll be a pretty lively corpse."

"First, we've got to convince Pettigrew and Yoeman to go along with this idea."

"We'd better be riding," Dusty said. "If we do move that money, we'll have to do it before morning."

Leaving his men to guard the camp, Wolfe rode back to town with Dusty and Hunch. There they roused Pettigrew out of bed and Wolfe explained the plan.

"Nobody's going to break into my vault," Pettigrew snapped grumpily.

"Just remember that we'll hold you personally responsible for any money those thieves take from your bank," Wolfe said.

Pettigrew frowned in the lamplight. The possibility of having to make up the loss of that money from his own account hit the banker hard.

"What makes you so sure they're going to try to rob the bank?"

"Didn't you see those tough hands riding in tonight?" Dusty asked.

"Well. I saw a couple of men go up to the saloon that I'd never seen before," Pettigrew admitted. "They did look like rough ones."

"There are a dozen like that in town right now," Dusty said.

"All right," Pettigrew said finally. "Get Fred Yoeman over here and we'll talk it over. He'll have to agree to having the money in his store."

"I'll get him," Dusty said.

Fred Yoeman was harder to wake up than Pettigrew had been and he resented the intrusion into his rest. But when Dusty told him that Pettigrew wanted him over at his place immediately, he dressed quickly and went with Dusty, grumbling with every step.

At Pettigrew's, Wolfe and Dusty explained the situation. Yoeman was easily convinced that the bank vault might not be burglar proof and agreed to letting the money be hidden in the back of his hardware store.

"I want it understood," he warned, "I'm not responsible for it just because it is in my store."

"You'll tell around town tomorrow morning that Wolfe was killed in that stampede out at his camp last night," Dusty said to Yoeman. "That will explain to everyone why he isn't at the school picnic. If he was dead, you'd be the one who would be sure to know it so you're the one to spread the word."

Yoeman nodded. "I'll take care of it. When do we move the money?"

"Right now," Dusty said. "It's got to be done before daylight."

"I'll have to have some light to see to open the vault," Pettigrew complained.

"We'll be mighty careful about any light in the bank," Dusty said. "Won't make any difference if there is a light in the back of the hardware. When Fred tells people that Vyrl Wolfe is dead, they'll just think Fred was fitting him into a coffin during the night. We'll set the time for the funeral for tomorrow afternoon after the school program."

"Do you figure the crisis will be over by then?" Pettigrew asked.

"Maybe," Dusty said. "I expect this gang to hit the town while everybody is at the school program and picnic. If they don't, we can go ahead with the fake funeral and Wolfe can guard the money in the hardware store until this gang either tries to rob the bank or leaves town."

"It's two thirty now," Yoeman said. "We'd better get busy."

Yoeman went down to his store and opened the back door and lighted a lamp. Wolfe went with him and stretched out on a table there, just in case someone got curious about the light and peeked in.

Dusty went with Pettigrew and Hunch to the back door of the bank and there Pettigrew unlocked the door and they slipped quietly inside. Pettigrew found a candle and Dusty made a shield from two boxes to keep any light from reaching the street windows.

Pettigrew quickly spun the dial on the vault and got the big door open. In a short time, he had put all the money that had come in on the stage plus much of his own reserve into four canvas bags. Dusty and Hunch each took two and Pettigrew locked the vault again.

Blowing out the candle, they felt their way to the back door and out into the alley. Pettigrew locked the rear door of the bank then they moved silently up the alley.

Dusty kept his eyes moving. This was the dangerous part of the scheme. If anyone had seen them coming from the bank, they'd quickly figure out what was happening. They could grab this money now with little risk. But nothing stirred and Dusty was sure they had not been noticed. Once inside the hardware store, they put the money down and Hunch hurried back outside to stand guard while Dusty and Yoeman found a place to hide the money.

"Safest place I can think of is right in this coffin

you've made," Dusty said. "You always line the coffins with muslin, don't you? Put the money in first, then stretch the muslin over it. Nobody's liable to find it there."

Yoeman nodded. "You're right. And if anybody wonders why I've got the muslin already in the coffin, I can tell them I've got a funeral today."

"Better make sure nobody gets close enough to see that much," Dusty suggested. "They'd want to see the body then."

Yoeman jerked a thumb at Wolfe. "I've got it if they insist."

Dusty grinned. "Lets hope nobody wants to see it."

"I'll stay right in this room until we're sure the money is safe," Wolfe said. "Got an extra rifle, Fred?"

"Sure," Yoeman said. "Got lots of them in the store. I'll get one for you with plenty of ammunition. I'll also bring you some breakfast in the morning."

"You'd better have a grave dug in case we have to go through with the fake funeral," Dusty said. "Now let's get to bed. Must be after three."

He and Hunch cut across lots beside Yoeman's barn and his house and on to Molly's boarding house. They slipped in quietly, careful not to wake the sleepers. But Dusty found it hard to sleep. It had been a long hard day. And the one coming up would certainly be no better.

Dusty and Hunch ate breakfast with the other boarders and Molly even commented on the fact that they had decided to be civilized for a change. When

Jennie headed over to the school house to finish preparations for the program, Dusty went with her.

"I'd like to borrow a couple of your pigeons," he said.

"What for?" she demanded. "I want those pigeons here. The children are proud of them and will want to show them off to their parents."

"I only need two," Dusty said. "If I'm guessing right, they could be back here in time for the parents to see them."

"You won't tell me what you want them for?" Jennie asked.

"It would sound ridiculous," Dusty said. "Besides, a secret that everybody knows is no secret. The pigeons won't be hurt; I'll promise that."

Reluctantly, Jennie took two of the five pigeons out of their cages and gave them to Dusty. Dusty thanked her and hurried down the street to the bank.

"Got a deposit for your vault," he told Pettigrew who had just opened the bank.

Pettigrew stared at the pigeons and shook his head. "Not in my bank."

"They're homing pigeons," Dusty explained. "Their roost is at the school house. We'll put these in the vault. If anybody opens the vault while we are at the program or picnic, these pigeons will come to the school house. We'll know then that somebody is in here."

Pettigrew nodded in approval and quickly opened the vault. Dusty put the pigeons inside.

167

The program was set for ten o'clock with the picnic scheduled for noon. Dusty and Hunch went over to the school house just before ten, Hunch carrying his accordion. It looked to Dusty as if everybody in town and the surrounding country was there.

As the program got under way, Dusty checked the crowd. Everyone he knew in town was there except Sitzman and Gumpy. Dusty was sure now that he had guessed right. If Sitzman and Gumpy weren't planning some mischief during the activities at the school house, they would surely be here themselves. Every business place in town had closed for the program.

Dusty enjoyed the program. Jennie handled it well, he thought. But he kept one eye cocked toward town. At any minute he expected to see the two pigeons winging their way back to their cages at the school house.

Hunch played several numbers on his accordion. Dusty couldn't see anything so great about the music since he'd heard those tunes over and over as he and Hunch rode the miles together. But it was new to the people here and they insisted on several encores.

Then the program was over and there was a rush by the women to get the picnic dinner ready. Dusty congratulated Jennie on a fine program.

"Where are my pigeons?" she asked. "Right after dinner, the children will want to show them to their parents."

"If they're not back by then," Dusty said. "I'll go get them."

Jennie frowned. "Where have you put them?"

"In a safe place," Dusty said, his eyes scanning the town.

Dusty and Hunch ate together and had just finished their dinner when Dusty's attention was caught by the flap of white wings. He grabbed Hunch's arm.

"Here come the pigeons."

"Somebody is in the bank. What do we do now?"

"Round up Pettigrew and Yoeman and all of Wolfe's men that are here," Dusty said. "When Sitzman's men find the vault is empty, they'll probably start looking for the money."

Dusty quickly made the rounds of the men, telling each one what had happened. They got up and took their plates to the end of the table, whether they were through eating or not. Jennie was sitting on a bench brought out from the school house and Dusty stopped there before heading for town.

"Your pigeons are back," he said softly. "Better put them in their cages."

"Where do we go?" Pettigrew asked when Dusty joined the men a short distance from the school house.

"To the hardware store," Dusty said. "If the gang has given up and left town, that's fine. But if they're looking for that money, we may have to put up a fight."

Dusty led the men down the side street then into the alley behind the bank. At the rear of the hardware store, Yoeman unlocked the door while Dusty ran down the alley-way to the street.

Dusty took one peek at the street and realized his worst fears. He saw Sitzman and Gumpy over by the saloon. But there were nearly a dozen well armed men going along the street. As Dusty looked, one man broke the lock on the barber shop across the street and went inside. They were looking for the money they knew should have been in the bank vault. They'd go through every building in town unless they found it.

Hurrying back to the rear door of the hardware store, he went inside and faced the men waiting there.

"They're searching every building in town," he said. "They'll soon be here."

"We can hold them off," said Wolfe, confidently.

Dusty shook his head. "I'm not so sure. There are nearly a dozen of them. They've got us outnumbered and they're tough gun hands."

"We've got to protect this money," Pettigrew said.

"That may be easier said than done," Yoeman said, fear in his voice.

XVII

"We can't just stand here!" Pettigrew shouted excitedly. "Let's do something."

"What?" Wolfe asked. "Do you want us to run off and leave this money for them?"

"No, no," Pettigrew shouted. "We've got to defend this place."

"We will," Dusty said. "Come on, Fred. Let's meet them when they come in."

Dusty and Fred Yoeman went through the partition door into the main part of the store. They had barely gotten there when a man started battering the door. Yoeman yelled that he'd open the door and the hammering stopped.

Yoeman hurried to the front of the store and unlocked the door. Two men were standing there.

"What do you want?" Yoeman demanded with as much courage as he could muster.

"We're going to search your store," one man said. "You've got some money hidden somewhere."

"Not here," Yoeman said. "I run a hardware store."

"How about the back?" one man asked. He had a gun held loosely in his hand.

"I've got a coffin back there with a body ready to be buried."

"We'll just take a look," one of the men said, and stepped inside the door.

"Don't you have any respect for the dead?" Dusty asked.

The man stared at Dusty. He evidently had not seen him in the dim interior before. His eyes brightened when he saw the marshal's badge. "So you're Marshal Dusty Dekin," he said slowly. "We've got orders to kill you on sight. That means right now."

Dusty heard a gun cock behind him and Hunch's voice came out of the doorway.

"Try it, mister, and you're a dead man. We've got a dozen guns trained on you."

The man squinted through the gloomy interior of the

store and his ears told him what his eyes probably couldn't. Dusty heard the guns cocking behind him, too. The man had started to raise his gun but now he stopped.

"So you've got an army behind you. There'll be another time."

The two men quickly backed out of the door and Yoeman slammed it shut. The men poured out of the back room.

"They know we're here now," Wolfe said. "When they don't find the money any other place, they'll figure it is here. Can we hold them off?"

Dusty shook his head. "I doubt it. They might even set fire to the place if they can't rout us out any other way."

"Wish the rest of my men were here," Wolfe said.

"Somebody had to guard your camp out there," Dusty said. "Let me think a minute. We're supposed to have a funeral this afternoon. In fact, it is about time for it. Did you get the grave dug?" Dusty looked at Yoeman.

Yoeman nodded. "Sure. I had a couple of boys dig it this morning. I didn't check to see how deep they dug it. Didn't figure on using it."

"Maybe we will," Dusty said. "Those men out there may not have any respect for the dead but they're superstitious enough that they won't interfere with a funeral procession."

"What good is a funeral going to do us?" Pettigrew asked.

Wolfe grinned. "I think I know. The body we bury will be the money."

"Wait a minute," Hunch objected. "They said they were out to kill Dusty. If we take a coffin out of here, we'll have to have pall bearers. That won't leave enough men to protect Dusty. They'll kill him while we bury the money."

"Not if I'm in the coffin," Dusty said.

"We ain't burying you alive," Hunch objected.

"I hope not," Dusty agreed. "Once we get to the cemetery, you can let me out. Pick six men to carry the coffin. Hunch, you take the spot nearest my head. You can keep me posted on what is happening. I'll listen for your voice."

"That might work," Wolfe said. "But what about me? If Sitzman and Gumpy see me, they'll know I'm not dead and the funeral is a fake."

Dusty nodded. "I've been thinking about that. Somebody has to go to the livery barn for a team and wagon to haul the coffin to the cemetery. While those men are going out the front, you can go out the back." He peered through the small dingy rear window. "I see only two men out there and they're both strangers. They won't recognize you, Vyrl. You pretend to be scared to death."

"I won't have to pretend," Wolfe said. "They'll probably shoot me on sight."

"Not if you go out with your hands up. They'll grab you and search you. You tell them you're getting out while you can. They'll let you go because that means one less gun for them to fight in here. You can wait at the boarding house."

Wolfe nodded. Two of Wolfe's men were dispatched through the front door to go to the livery barn for the team and wagon. Wolfe burst out the back door with his hands up. The two gunmen out there reacted just as Dusty had guessed they would. After searching Wolfe, they let him go and he hurried across the lots toward the boarding house without letting himself be seen from the street.

Dusty moved to the front room and watched out the window. The two men were not disturbed as they went to the livery barn and got the team and wagon. They drove it back to the hardware store and Dusty went into the back room.

"Hope this thing won't suffocate me," he said as he gingerly climbed into the coffin.

"It won't," Yoeman said. "While you were out there, I bored a couple of small holes just below the lid to let air in. The money is still under the muslin."

Dusty stretched out, using a small pillow Yoeman gave him to absorb some of the jolts on his head. He made sure Hunch was stationed nearest to his head, then Yoeman clapped the lid on the coffin and nailed it down with small tacks.

"Reckon you can bust out of there if you have to," he said. "I guess we're ready."

It was almost pitch black inside the coffin. The holes Yoeman had drilled in the sides just above Dusty's head did let in a little light but the muslin filtered out most of it.

174

He felt himself being lifted and carried. He could mark the progress by the sound of the boots thumping on the board floor of the store. Then the first men stepped off the porch and Dusty felt himself slide forward as the coffin tipped. Then there was a jolt as one end of the coffin was dropped on the back of the wagon and then slid forward.

"Everything is going just as you thought," Hunch said softly and Dusty was surprised how well he could hear.

The jolt of the wagon as the team started toward the cemetery was the hardest part for Dusty. Not only was the ride rough but the money under the muslin made lumps that gouged Dusty's back.

"Sitzman and Gumpy are watching," Hunch reported. "But they're not following. Most of Sitzman's men are standing just outside the hardware. You can bet they're going to go through that store just as soon as we're out of sight."

"Did all of Wolfe's men come?" Dusty asked softly.

At first he thought Hunch hadn't heard him, then his voice came through again a little louder than before. Apparently they were farther from Sitzman's men.

"They're all trailing the wagon. But we've got more trouble. We've just turned up the side street toward the cemetery. Somebody at the school house saw us and now everybody there is coming out to the cemetery for the burying. How about that?"

"Somebody will have to conduct a little service," Dusty said. "Then people will go home. After they're gone, I'll get out."

"I just hope they do go home soon. We'll get Ed Klosson to say something. He was the one who hired Vyrl Wolfe. He's coming from the school house now."

Ed Klosson was a good choice, Dusty thought. Klosson didn't know that Vyrl Wolfe wasn't dead and in this coffin. So he should do a better job than someone who knew that any eulogy he said would be heard by the corpse.

"We're almost there," Hunch said after a long time.

Dusty was glad to hear that. He had bruises all over his body from the jolting ride.

The wagon finally stopped and the coffin was slid to the back of the wagon. This was the place where Dusty had hoped his ordeal would end but now he knew it wouldn't. The people from the school house would stay until somebody said something over the coffin. That meant that the ropes to let the coffin into the grave would have to be stretched over the hole and the casket set on them.

He felt the coffin being lifted and moved. Then he felt it sway as it was set down on the ropes. This was going a little farther than he had bargained for.

He heard somebody saying something but the man was too far from Dusty's prison for him to hear what it was. He decided it must be Ed Klosson. Then from directly above him, he heard Hunch's voice again. It was little more than a whisper.

"Sitzman and his men are coming. They must have searched the hardware. Maybe they've guessed that the money is in the coffin."

Dusty considered that. If it was so, there was no telling what Sitzman's men might do.

"They stopped at the edge of the crowd," Hunch whispered. "What do we do now?"

Dusty thought about answering Hunch. But what if somebody was near enough to hear a voice coming from the coffin? He could imagine what would happen. There was only one thing they could do now, Dusty thought. They had to go on with the sham.

"Go ahead," he whispered, low enough that no one could hear unless he was very close to the coffin.

He wasn't sure that Hunch had heard but then he felt the coffin begin going down. It seemed to Dusty that it had been sinking long enough to be in a hole thirty feet deep before it hit bottom. The ropes sung as they were pulled out from under the coffin. He was in the grave now. All that was left to complete the burial was to shovel in the dirt.

A few lumps of dirt thudded on the coffin and some words were being said at the top of the grave. "Dust to dust—" Dusty imagined he heard.

He felt a touch of panic. This was too real. Then there was a heavy thud on the coffin lid followed by Hunch's voice.

"Most of the people have left but Sitzman's men are still out there. We can't fight them off so we're going to have to bury you. I'm putting big chunks of sod from the lid to the wall so the dirt won't filter down over those air holes. You'll have all the air trapped in that side pocket beside the coffin. We'll get you out as soon as that gang of cut-throats leave."

Dusty heard something being shoved around on the coffin lid then a grunt as Hunch was lifted out. The dirt began to rain down on the coffin and the sharp thud of it changed to soft thumps as dirt began hitting dirt instead of wood. Dusty had never felt so alone and helpless in his life.

Then—mercy of mercies—he heard scraping sounds. And—free!—he was looking up at Hunch's grinning face.

"We thought those gun hands were never going to leave," Hunch said. "Did you almost smother?"

"I've had fresher air to breathe," Dusty said. "Are you sure they're not watching us now?"

"We've got two men down at the edge of town watching. Sitzman's men all went back to the saloon, apparently sure that we were going to bury the coffin and leave it. But I'm positive they suspect that the money is in there."

"I've got an idea," Dusty said. "Hunch, is your accordion here?"

"Sure. What would you like to hear?"

"Oh, come on!"

Dusty ordered, "Somebody get down there and get that money. If we're sure Sitzman's outfit isn't watching, we'll take the money out and hide it right now."

One of the men dropped down into the coffin and tore away the muslin, handing up the sacks of money. Not far away was the dirt left over from the last burial in the cemetery. Dusty took a shovel and led the way to this pile of dirt. Shoveling away some of the dirt, he pushed the sacks of money into the hole and scooped the dirt back over them and tamped it in. Unless spying eyes had seen the money buried there, no one was liable to find it.

Hunch came back with his accordion. Dusty reached for it and asked for some rope.

"Don't you damage my accordion," Hunch warned.

"This won't hurt it," Dusty promised. "I just want to make sure we know exactly when they get this coffin open. It may be pretty dark when they dig it up."

Fastening one end of the accordion to the bottom of the coffin, he tied a short rope to the other end and fastened that to the lid of the coffin. When the lid was put down on the coffin, the accordion would be squeezed together. But when the lid was raised, the accordion would be stretched out and that would make a squall that was a familiar sound to Dusty and Hunch.

"Quite an alarm," one man said approvingly.

Dusty got out of the grave and stepped away—then stopped as he saw a large bull-snake slithering through the grass.

"Didn't somebody tell me that Sitzman is deathly afraid of snakes?" he asked.

"I heard he nearly killed Gumpy once because he showed him a snake," one man said. "I guess he almost had a heart attack."

With a little help, Dusty caught the snake and dropped him into the coffin before he lowered the lid.

"We'd better get this grave filled fast," Dusty said. "If we don't get back into town pretty soon, they'll get suspicious."

"If they catch us still filling this grave, somebody will have to dig graves for all of us," Hunch predicted.

XVIII

They finished filling the grave without an alarm being sounded by the guards. As they started toward town, Hunch moved up beside Dusty.

"You'd better make yourself hard to find," he said when they were almost in town. "Sitzman's men have orders to shoot you on sight, you know."

Dusty nodded. "Here comes someone else who would like nothing better than to see me dead, too." He pointed to three men coming down the side street, obviously hurrying to meet them.

"Now what do you suppose they want?" Pettigrew asked worriedly.

"Trouble, more than likely," one of Wolfe's men said.

Dusty watched them come: Craig Usta; the deputy, Zeke Torberg; and Usta's best gunman, Ben Lozar. They didn't appear to be bent on trouble although the anger in Usta's face was obvious.

"What's chawing on you?" Fred Yoeman asked, looking to the men around him to back him up.

"That bunch of gun slicks broke into Nettles' safe and got our money," Usta said. "Did they get yours, too?"

"They tried," Pettigrew said. "They got into my safe, all right. But we had taken the money out."

"Looks like you win with your dam then," Usta said bitterly.

"We haven't gotten rid of Sitzman's gang yet," Dusty said.

Ed Klosson, who had stayed to help fill the grave and had been brought up to date on what had happened, spoke up. "You know who has your money. Why don't you send your gunmen after it?"

"I know some of those gun slingers Sitzman has," Ben Lozar said quickly. "I'm not bucking a stacked deck."

"Looks like we're in the same boat," Dusty said. "Sitzman's men are still here, aren't they?"

"In the saloon," Usta said. "Don't know what they're hanging around for."

"We know," Dusty said. "They aim to make another try at getting the money from the bank. I just thought of something. You want your money back and the farmers want to keep theirs. If you'll team up, you might both get what you want."

Usta frowned. "How do you figure that?"

"Sitzman doesn't intend to leave until he gets the bank money. If you and Klosson will join your outfits, you might be able to trap Sitzman's men. If you can, you stand a good chance of getting your money back, as well as saving the bank's money."

"Watch for a trick," Lozar warned Usta.

The rancher scratched his head, ignoring Lozar.

"Sounds reasonable," he said finally. "We sure ain't got nothing to lose. How about it, Klosson?"

Klosson nodded his head. "We've got plenty to lose and we'll probably lose it, too, if we try bucking those gunmen alone. But with your help, we just might succeed."

Usta, all business, turned to Dusty. "This is your idea. How do you figure to pull it off?"

"First, let's go to Yoeman's hardware store. That's right across from the saloon. We can watch Sitzman's outfit from there. I don't figure they'll try anything until after dark but if they do, we've got to know it."

XIX

Dusty's eyes had been straining into the darkness. Then he saw Sitzman and his men—almost at the cemetery.

"How do we get that guard?" Hunch whispered after Sitzman had led the rest of his men into the cemetery.

"Surprise him with this sawed-off shotgun," Dusty whispered. "He won't know I won't use it on him."

Quietly, Dusty inched his way toward the guard. He was within five feet of him before the guard realized that he wasn't alone. He wheeled, swinging up his gun but he froze when he found himself staring into the twin snub barrels of Dusty's shotgun.

"Not a peep out of you," Dusty whispered. "Come over here."

The man meekly followed Dusty's orders, dropping

his gun on command. Hunch scooped it up. Back a few feet from the gate, Dusty picked up some of the rope they had brought from Yoeman's Hardware and tied up the guard then gagged him. He heard no sound from the east rim of the cemetery. Either the men there hadn't tried to capture the guards or had done a quiet job of it.

Out in the cemetery, someone had lit a lantern so the men could see what they were doing. Dusty watched them work by the weird flickering light. The dirt flew as the men took turns with the shovels.

Dusty heard the first crunch as a shovel hit the wooden lid of the coffin. It sounded entirely different from this angle than it had when he'd been underneath.

Then the dirt was out and one man began to loosen the nails holding down the lid. Dusty could almost picture the men ringing the cemetery, waiting tensely.

Then the lid came up and the accordion groaned as air wheezed into it. Even when he was expecting it, Dusty realized that was a horrible sound to be coming from the depths of a grave.

The men who had been crowding around the grave fell back as though the devil himself had leaped out of the grave at them. Several of them broke into wild runs, going in every direction. Two came down the road toward the gate. When they reached the gate, they were halted abruptly by Dusty and his sawed-off shotgun.

"That will be far enough," Dusty said softly. "Drop

your guns and get over there." He motioned toward Hunch.

The men were too terrified to disobey. Hunch and Dusty had them tied up before one of the men managed to mutter, "What is in that grave?"

"That was the soul of the departed complaining about being disturbed," Dusty said solemnly.

He looked back out at the grave site. Only six men remained. There seemed to be no more movement around the cemetery than there had been. Either the frightened gunmen had escaped or had been captured the same as Dusty had caught the two heading out the gate.

Sitzman's voice was dominating the scene out at the grave. "You bunch of lily-livered cowards!" he yelled. "Afraid of your own shadows! That's just a trick they pulled to scare us away."

"You think the money is in there?" Gumpy asked.

"Sure it is," Sitzman said. "Why else would they rig up that squeeze box to scare the daylights out of us?"

Hunch snickered and Dusty nudged him to silence.

"Bring that light over here," Sitzman snapped at the man with the lantern. "I'm going to get down there and get that money."

"What about the fellows who ran?" one man asked.

"They just ran away from their share of this money," Sitzman snapped. "The cowards!"

The man with the lantern came back to the grave reluctantly. Sitzman prepared to swing himself down into the grave as the lantern came closer. He had a hand on either side of the grave and was lowering himself when the light reached into the coffin and he saw the bull snake coiled in one end of the coffin.

With a scream that would have done credit to a freight engine, Sitzman swung himself out of the grave, rolling ten feet from the hole. He came to his feet screaming and cursing. Gumpy ran over, trying to calm him.

"What happened?" Gumpy demanded.

"You did it!" Sitzman screamed crazily. "You put that snake there!" Sitzman clawed for the gun at his hip.

Gumpy fell back. "I couldn't have. I just got here. I didn't even see any snake."

Gumpy began babbling wildly, stumbling backward, as he realized that Sitzman was out of his mind.

"You did it!" Sitzman screamed again. "I told you I'd kill you if you ever scared me with another snake."

Too late the other men realized what Sitzman was going to do. They lunged at him just as he fired. Dusty saw Gumpy twist around and fall then the other men were wrestling with Sitzman. Sitzman struggled to get free, trying to turn the gun on Gumpy for another shot.

In the struggle, the men stumbled back until they were on the edge of the grave again. Suddenly Sitzman lost his balance on the lip of the hole. His hands flew into the air as he tried to keep falling. His scream ripped the night like a piercing knife.

The other men fell back from him as he flailed the air to keep his balance. For what seemed like a full minute to Dusty, Sitzman teethered on the brink of the grave then he went over backward into the grave, his terrified scream sinking with him.

Suddenly everything was quiet. Dusty expected to see Sitzman scrambling wildly out of the grave. But nothing happened. Dusty suddenly realized that they'd never have a better chance to gain an advantage over Sitzman's men than right now.

Leaping to his feet, he led Hunch in a charge toward the grave. Other men, seeing Dusty, rushed in from all sides of the cemetery. The four men still standing at the grave seemed stunned by what had happened and they dropped their guns without any resistance.

Dusty took the lantern from the man holding it and moved to the grave. Sitzman was crumpled crossways across the top of the box. He wasn't moving. A couple of Usta's men climbed down and lifted the gambler out. Dusty felt for his pulse and was astonished when he found none. Sitzman was dead.

"Scared to death by a snake," one man breathed.

"I knew he had heart trouble," another said. "But letting a snake scare him to death—"

Dusty checked Gumpy and found that Sitzman's shot had only broken a shoulder. Gumpy got to his feet, holding his right arm with his left hand.

"We caught most of the men who ran when that accordion squalled," one of Usta's men said.

"That about takes care of Sitzman's gang," Dusty said. "Let's get our money then go down and see if we can find the money that they took from Nettles' safe."

Grabbing a shovel, Dusty headed for the mound of dirt where he had buried the bank money while someone climbed back down and got Hunch's accordion, some the worse from having helped break Sitzman's fall into the grave.

Dusty knew before he reached the pile of dirt that something was wrong. There was a hole where the money should have been.

"Who could have stolen it?" Yoeman asked in disbelief. "This gang sure didn't."

"I think I know," Dusty said and turned toward the gate of the cemetery on the run.

He wasn't just sure where to look. Pettigrew was the only one not accounted for who knew where the money had been hidden. Dusty had to find him now.

He was far ahead of the men herding the prisoners down from the cemetery when he passed Molly's boarding house. He headed for the bank, wondering if Pettigrew might have gone there. As he was passing the little barn behind the bank, he stopped suddenly as he heard angry voices.

He had to listen for only a few seconds to get the picture. Pettigrew was hitching his horse to his cart, apparently planning to take the money somewhere and hide it rather than put it back in the safe where others would learn that he had it. But Queeny had caught up with him and now she was demanding a cut of what he had taken.

"You won't get anything!" Pettigrew snapped, trying to hold his voice down.

"I told you I'd take my cut," Queeny said, making no effort to hold her voice low. "You can give it to me now or I'll let the whole town know you've got this money. And I'll tell a few other things, too."

"You won't tell anybody anything," Pettigrew said, his rage breaking through his caution.

Dusty ran around the corner of the barn. Queeny didn't sound like she knew she was in danger. Maybe she didn't believe the banker was capable of murder. Dusty did.

He charged through the door where a lantern was swinging from a wire above the stall. Pettigrew whirled around, furious at the interruption, then stopped in his tracks when he saw the short shotgun in Dusty's hands.

"I've got a place over in the jail for both of you," Dusty said. "Klosson will take care of that money."

"He stole the money," Queeny yelled. "You've got nothing on me."

"We'll let a judge decide that," Dusty said.

Pettigrew's fury suddenly broke. "Some of that money belongs to the bank," he whimpered.

"We'll figure out how much later on," Dusty said.

A half dozen men crowded into the barn behind Dusty, having come on ahead of those bringing in the prisoners. Ed Klosson and Zeke Torberg were among them. Dusty turned the money over to Klosson and told Torberg to put the two prisoners in his jail.

"My jail ain't going to hold all the people we've arrested," Torberg complained.

Dusty didn't wait to listen to Torberg's troubles. There was still the ranchers' money to locate. And if he was ever going to find out who had killed his father, tonight was the time to do it while everything was in such a turmoil that a secret was a hard thing to protect. Neither Sitzman nor Gumpy had been carrying Matt Dekin's watch tonight.

Outside, Dusty waited for the men coming from the cemetery. Gumpy should be the key to both the money and the watch and Hunch was herding him this way while Usta's men had the remainder of Sitzman's gang under their guns.

Usta's men stopped at the barn with their prisoners but Dusty motioned Hunch to prod Gumpy on then fell in step with his partner.

"Where are we going to take him?" Hunch asked.

"To the saloon," Dusty said. "That's where Sitzman's outfit holed up this afternoon. So the money they stole from Nettles' safe should be there. And I think Gumpy can tell us something about that watch we're looking for."

The light was dim but Dusty was sure he saw Gumpy's face twist in fear. Dusty and Hunch aimed for the saloon and Gumpy shuffled along ahead of them.

After unlocking the saloon door, Gumpy stopped. "I need a doc for this shoulder," he complained.

"Reckon you do," Dusty agreed. "As soon as you drag out the money you stole from Nettles' safe and give me that watch, we'll get you to a doc."

Gumpy grunted and went inside where Dusty lighted a lamp. Defiance was in Gumpy's face but the pain in his shoulder and Dusty's determination broke his resistance.

"You're going to kill me, anyway," he muttered.

He shuffled behind the bar and produced a box. Dusty knew it held the ranchers' money.

Then his eye fell on the watch lying beside the bar rag. He picked it up. "Who claims this?" he demanded.

"Serg owned that," Gumpy said reluctantly.

"How come it was here behind the bar?"

"I—he kept it here when he wasn't wearing it," Gumpy mumbled.

"You claimed it, didn't you?" Dusty demanded, grabbing Gumpy by the shirt front.

"I didn't kill Matt Dekin!" Gumpy cried hysterically. "Serg did that."

"But you helped him with the ambush."

Gumpy didn't deny it. Hunch jabbed a finger under the bartender's nose.

"Where's the money you stole from my pa?"

"Most of it is in a bank in Denver," Gumpy said. "We used some to buy this saloon."

"We'll let the law take care of you," Dusty said. "Hunch, looks like you own a saloon."

"Usta ain't going to stop us from getting in our dam," Ed Klosson declared.

"It ain't all one-sided," Usta growled. "We'll let them dirt farmers do the hard work of putting up the hay along the river. Then we'll buy it. That will leave us time to raise more cattle back in the hills."

But Dusty wasn't listening. Coming toward him, half at a run, was Jennie. And then they were in each other's arms.

Center Point Publishing
600 Brooks Road • PO Box 1
Thorndike ME 04986-0001 USA

(207) 568-3717

US & Canada:
1 800 929-9108